DON JUAN

BROTHERHOOD PROTECTORS WORLD

LEANNE TYLER

Twisted Page Press LLC

BROTHERHOOD PROTECTORS

ORIGINAL SERIES BY ELLE JAMES

To Shannon for your extra hard work on whipping this one into shape for me. Thanks for your editing talent.

CHAPTER 1

SIMONE REID UNLOCKED her apartment door and pulled her roll along straight into her bedroom. She kicked off her heels, shimmied out of her hose, and then stripped out of her business suit before she finally headed for the shower to wash the memory of a failed trip out of her mind. Typically she loved traveling for business, but she'd mixed personal affairs with work this time around and both had not gone well. She'd been so consumed trying to trail her father's last steps that she didn't spend enough time focusing on her client. She'd renewed the contract, but Webster-Reynolds had not been happy with her and she was certain her boss, Robert Cranston, would be hearing about it. She could kiss her upcoming promotion good-bye unless she knew of a way to convince her boss that being distracted trying to locate her father on company time was the best policy instead of requesting time off to do so.

She just had to hope and pray that her dad showed back up eventually and that no foul play was involved. If his business partners weren't concerned it was odd that he hadn't been seen in three weeks, then perhaps Simone was overreacting. Her dad was as much of a free-spirit as she was when it came to following his own path in life. He was a great salesman even if his tactics were sometimes brought into question. She was just glad his secretary had given her the location of the hotel where he'd been staying on his trip.

Turning off the water, Simone reached for the terry cloth towel and wrapped it around her body. She stepped out onto the memory foam bathmat and let her feet dry for a moment before she ran into her bedroom to quickly dress for a night out with her girlfriends. She needed to unwind and Carly's recent divorce was a great reason to celebrate. Checking the clock, she saw she had just enough time to touch up her hair and makeup and slip into a spring dress before Colleen would be texting that she was downstairs to pick her up.

So she pushed all thoughts of her dad's whereabouts and her job aside as she pulled on her dress before she rushed back into the bathroom. She applied fresh eye shadow, mascara and lipstick reminding herself she was going out with her friends tonight to have fun and who knew what else. She loved the possibilities on nights like this.

Her phone buzzed. Colleen's name flashed on her screen, so she dashed off a text to say she was on her way before she grabbed the small gift bag for Carly and headed out the door.

· · ·

MUSIC GREETED them as they entered the Pied Piper bar on the waterfront in downtown Chicago. Colleen had been Miss Chatty Cathy all the way there, while Carly had fidgeted with the zippers on her faux leather jacket in the backseat.

"Let's get this party started!" Simone raised her arms in the air, a tiger print gift bag in one hand, a wristlet dangling from the other as she made her way between the tables.

Colleen carried a small gift bag as well, and Carly followed with her large black purse that looked like an overnight bag. Good girl! Their last conversation about what this night could mean appeared to have stuck with her friend and Carly was following through. Even if she didn't look thrilled about it. *The girl needed to get laid, badly.*

Simone left her friends at the table and went to the eight by eight stage area and began dancing with the chrome pole. She loved the way her reddish-brown hair shimmered in the overhead spotlights and reflected in the mirrored wall. She soon got lost in the music as she danced, forgetting about the world around her as the rhythm consumed her, and she didn't come back to reality until she heard Carly tell the bartender, "Hit me again."

"Woohoo, that's the spirit!" Simone called. The more she swayed and shimmied, the higher her dress rose with each move. However, she was still dancing alone. She didn't understand why she wasn't drawing the attention of any of the men in the bar tonight.

Even Colleen over by the jukebox, swaying to the music with her blonde ponytail bobbing, was alone. Likewise, Jules lounged at the table by herself with her feet up, shaking her head to the music.

"You guys look like a hair color commercial," Carly said, laughing.

"Look who's talking." Jules turned in her direction and gestured with her drink. "You're the one who looks like something out of a Victoria's Secret catalog."

"What? I'm well covered. Besides, you all picked it out." Carly reached a hand to her shoulder length honey-blonde hair and smoothed the imaginary flyaway strands back into place. Then she rested her hand at her midriff where the white clinging tank stopped, exposing her tummy. A light-weight, faux-leather jacket covered the tank. The ensemble was finished off with matching black short shorts that covered all the essentials and did marvelous things for her legs. And, as if her legs weren't long enough, the black studded, open toe, mid-ankle boots she wore added three more inches to her height.

Simone left the pole and danced over to the bar, looking Carly in the eye. "The whole point of this evening is to get you out of your comfort zone. You're the one that wanted a change in your life. We wanted it to be a liberation, now that you're officially divorced from that control freak, Justin Porter."

Carly downed the next shot of tequila and set the glass back on the bar. "Another one, bartender."

Colleen rushed over to the bar, reaching for Carly's hand. "Pace yourself and don't forget to drink water. You don't want to find yourself flat on the floor," she warned with a sweet smile, leading her back to their table.

Simone followed with a pitcher of water and tray

containing the next round of drinks, which they toasted to Carly and her newfound freedom. When the next song began to play, Jules finally got to her feet and danced with Colleen and Simone. They urged Carly to join them, but she refused, deciding to sip water instead. A few frat boys from the University of Chicago joined them and they danced hard to the music. Simone even danced with a few of the executive types from downtown. That lasted until a hard and fast tempo song that she and Jules loved to jump around to begun to play and she left the guy behind to go find her friend. Jules was coming to find her as well. Colleen moved off to the side and took photos of them with her phone as usual, giggling.

When the song ended, the three headed back to the table and found Carly sitting there.

"What have you been up to?" Simone asked.

"Escaping the rough hands of the long-haired man at the bar. I've had enough shooters for one night."

"We need food." Colleen picked up the small menu on the table and rattled off the appetizers. "Let's get the slider platter and the loaded cheesy bacon fries."

"Girl, because you can eat like that and not gain an ounce doesn't mean we're all blessed with those genes," Simone said.

"Live a little." Jules snatched the menu from Colleen. "I'll go order and be right back with a round of beer for us all. Longnecks or a pitcher?"

"Longnecks."

Jules returned with four bottles.

"Let's toast Carly and her new life," Jules announced, handing out the bottles. "Isn't that what we're here for?"

"Here. Here." Colleen raised her bottle.

Carly blushed and tried to hide the fact by drinking her beer.

The waitress came shortly after with the sliders and the fries. The four talked, scarfed down the food, and then it was finally time to shower Carly with naughty gifts.

Simone squealed, stomping her feet happily on the floor as she produced the small tiger print grift bag with black tissue paper. "I hope you have lots of fun with these."

Carly actually eyed the bag as if she were afraid to reach inside, but finally she stuck her hand in and pulled out furry, leopard print handcuffs. "Oh. Well. Uh. Yea."

"This one's from me," Colleen said, sitting down another small, sparkly gift bag with bright tissue paper.

"Is there a theme to these gifts?" Carly asked.

"Yeah, that you use them," Simone said, feeling upset by her reaction to her gift.

The girls giggled as Carly reached inside and pulled out a handful of glow in the dark condoms. Her hand was suspended above the bag for a few seconds before she exclaimed a startled, "Oh!" and she dropped them back inside.

Flushed, Carly set aside Colleen's gift and reached for Jules's sedate white gift bag with pink tissue.

"Do I even want to look inside this one? It looks all innocent, but that means it's deceptive because it's coming from you, counselor."

Jules shrugged. "Depends on how adventurous you are."

Simone couldn't help but roll her eyes at that dead giveaway.

Taking a deep breath, Carly pulled out the pink tissue and unwrapped a biker babe leather thong teddy and whip set. "Good heavens!"

The girls laughed some more as Carly's cheeks flamed and she wrapped the items back in the tissue and stuffed them into the gift bag again. She put the other two gift bags inside of Jules's and then stowed the gifts inside her large black bag that contained a change of clothes in case she didn't go home tonight.

"You guys didn't have to do this or bring these here... tonight. You could have given them to me at my apartment."

Colleen shook her head. "That place is so small. I swear, my linen closet is bigger."

Simone snorted, made a face, and then covered her nose and mouth with both hands.

"Sorry you don't approve, but it was all I could afford. I wasn't awarded alimony."

"Which is asinine!" Jules stood up. "That is the one thing about your divorce I don't agree with. How could the judge grant it without awarding your alimony? Justin Porter comes from money. Didn't one of his ancestors found that country club he belongs to?"

Carly nodded. "One of the first members. But his family doesn't like to brag."

Simone snorted again. "Is that why he mentioned it so often when you were first dating?"

"Did he?"

"Yes." Jules tossed a used napkin on the table. "He got

the house. While you moved into a tiny apartment that you barely can afford without any support. You have no job. Your parents aren't speaking to you because you left him, it's—"

"I have a job interview next week now that everything is settled and I can focus on not going to court every day."

"Speaking of injustice, the legal system is screwy. Where is justice in the world?" Jules continued to fume.

Colleen patted their friend on the shoulder. "It'll be okay. The youth center will find money somewhere to support the programs for the kids. There have been budget cuts before and the center has survived."

Jules kicked the leg of a nearby chair. "Not like these cuts."

"I'm sorry, Jules. I hadn't realized it had gotten so bad this week," Simone said, feeling bad she hadn't been there for her friend. "Someone should have let me know when I got back in town from my business trip."

Jules shook her head. "Enough about me. It's Carly's night out and we still have plenty of time before the bar closes. Another round of drinks? A round of pool?"

"A little pole dancing for our divorcee?" Simone suggested, getting to her feet and trying to persuade Carly to join her up on the stage. "You're not going to find Mr. Right Now if you stay hidden behind a table all night. You gotta get out on the dance floor and move your moneymaker."

Carly shook her head and held up her hands. "Guys, please, stop. I think I've had more than my limit of alcohol for one night and dancing when I'm feeling like this is not going to be good. I won't attract anything but a bucket and a mop."

"Okay, then what would you like to do?" Colleen asked, reaching out and taking her hands in hers. "We're here to please."

"I want to spend time with my besties. Is that so wrong? I know you think I need to have a hot night out, but have I drawn a man to me tonight? Well, other than Mr. Longhair tattoo guy, but you know. Have either of you been propositioned? No. Is there something wrong with us?"

"I think we're sending off the wrong vibes," Colleen said. "We're woman, hear us roar, but stand your distance buster."

Jules smirked. "You got that right."

"More the reason we need to get up on the stage and shake our booties." Simone left the table, went to the juke box and selected *Firefly* and went to the stage and proceeded to sway and gyrate.

Colleen ran to join Simone, laughing. They joined hands, raising their arms in a slow motion wave. Soon Jules and Carly joined in. It wasn't long until a few of the guys in the bar sauntered over and began dancing as well.

Simone felt as if she were about to drop when the last song ended and the four of them headed back to the table. It had been just the release she needed. She hurried over to Carly and ribbed her about the frat boy she'd been dancing with.

"Woohoo, looks like Carly found her a young one." Simone hovered near her shoulder.

"He's not my type."

"Do you even know what your type is anymore?"

Carly shrugged.

A bell rang near the bar and everyone stopped what they were doing. The bartender climbed up on the wooden surface and announced, "Last call of the night. We'll be closing in fifteen."

Wolf howls and cheering came from the group of Frat boys and then a round of slaps on the backs of some of the guys.

"Wonder what that was all about?" Jules arched a brow. "Well, I hate to bail, but I have an early morning meeting."

"On a Saturday?" Simone questioned, wondering if Jules was just ditching them early like she normally did on Fridays.

Jules nodded. "With all the budget cuts, we have to figure out how we're going to keep the few programs we can from tanking."

It was clear from the sad face Colleen made before hugging Jules that she bought into it. "See you. Call if you need to talk." When she pulled away she looked at Carly and Simone. "I need to hit the ladies before we leave."

"Okay. We'll wait for you at the bar," Carly told her. Then she leaned toward Simone.

"I want to thank the bartender for cutting me off earlier. He saved me from making a fool out of myself."

"Are you sure that is the only reason you are wanting to talk to him?" Simone cooed.

She ignored her and slid onto one of the empty barstools.

"Come back for another shot?" the bartender asked.

"No. This girl knows when she's had her limit. You

were right to cut me off when you did. I wanted to thank you for doing that earlier. I'm Carly, by the way."

"Phil. And it was my pleasure to give you an out to get away from that guy. I could tell you didn't look comfortable with him touching you."

"No, I didn't. Thanks again."

"Are you single?" Simone asked. "Carly's recently divorced."

"Nope." Phil held up his olive toned hand sporting a wide titanium band on it.

"You'll have to excuse my friend here, she doesn't think before she speaks when she's been drinking."

"That's okay. It happens all the time in my line of work." Phil walked away to take care of a server at the other end of the bar.

"Too bad he's taken. He's hot. I'd do him in a heartbeat," Simone said, her libido kicking into override from the adrenaline rush of dancing.

"There isn't much you wouldn't do when you've been drinking."

"Ouch. Let's not get our claws out. I'm just trying to have some fun. Lighten up. Where'd fun Carly go all of a sudden?"

Carly glanced at her. "Sorry, but it's late and I'm getting a headache. I'm not accustomed to having all this kind of *fun*."

The door to the bar opened and a young leather clad man with a red rolled bandana tied around his dark head strode into the bar. He was followed by two more in jeans and dark t-shirts. All three had snake tattoo markings up and down their arms and necks that anyone in the city knew cried gang relations. It wasn't clear what their purpose was coming into the bar so late, nor did they approach Phil to order a drink. They meandered around as if they were interested in the juke box and maybe getting a table.

"We better get out of here." Simone grabbed Carly's arm and pulled her off the bar stool, but Carly shook her head.

"We can't, we're waiting on Colleen."

Simone started to protest but it died on her lips and came out more like a mouse's high pitched squeak when the trio headed back toward the bar.

"What can I do for you fellas?" Phil asked.

"Your money." The guy in the leather pulled a .45 on Phil.

Simone lowered her arms, letting her wristlet hang down so she could get her phone out of the pocket.

"Excuse me?" Phil didn't flinch. He remained calm despite the gun pointed at his face.

"Your money, mother fucker. Open up that fucking drawer and give us all your money or you and the rest of these assholes are dead."

The other two pulled out their guns as well and began waving them around to show they meant business. One pointed his shiny silver .45 at Simone and pulled the trigger, but a bullet didn't fire.

Simone cried out in alarm, dropping behind the bar. She tried to slow her racing heart as she repeated to herself that she was okay. She was alive. The bastard hadn't shot her. He was an insane freak, laughing his ass off for pointing the gun at her and pulling that trigger, but she'd have the last laugh when the police showed up. She slipped the wristlet off and freed her phone from the pocket so she could call 9-1-1.

She was trembling so bad it took what seemed forever for her to press the numbers on her display and the phone to register it. She had only gotten the 9-1 pressed when she heard the whack of something and then a gunshot, followed by breaking glass. Sucking in her breath she pressed the last digit and leaned forward to cover the phone as she slipped it up to her ear.

It was hard to hear what the 9-1-1 operator said because screams ricocheted throughout the place, mingled with the continued laughter from the shooter. Plus, Carly dropped to the floor beside her and sucked in a breath when she saw her on the phone. She gave her a thumbs up before she went crawling away. Simone pivoted on her knees wondering where her friend thought she was going until she saw her slip through the opening in the bar.

Simone quickly told the operator what was going on, where they were and that there was a live shooter, hiding her face when the gunman came around the side of the bar calling for Carly to stop and get away from the body or he'd shoot.

"Stay on the line, ma'am. You don't have to speak. I can hear you're in danger," the operator said. "I have officers in route to your location. They should be there any moment."

"Thank you," Simone whispered, closing her eyes.

She heard another whack, foul cursing and a thud.

Several heartbeats later she slowly rose to her feet and peered over the bar.

Carly stood in a pool of Phil's blood, holding the baseball bat to her side, but the gunman was on the ground, out cold.

"Damn, Carly, what have you done?"

CHAPTER 2

Liam Donovan watched his buddies, Will McLeod and Wyatt Kincaid, gather the last of their gear as he placed items in the proper spot in each tactical bag. It was the way their team leader, former Devgru SEAL Brand Chambers, liked it and he didn't want to upset the man. They'd had a good week in Chicago promoting the Brotherhood Protectors to the Chicago PD, which included a former Seal buddy of Brand's who was now a commander. It was another way that Hank Patterson, their boss, was trying to get his brain child, the Brotherhood Protectors and the wounded warriors he recruited for the job, back into everyday society.

Liam didn't mind being away from Eagle Rock, Montana. He'd only called the location in the Crazy Mountains home for a short time, but when an assignment was up he was always ready to hit the road.

Brand was the same way. He could tell by the way his buddy was pacing the floor that he was biding the time until the team could be on the way to the airport. Liam watched his leader head over to speak to Commander Burns, otherwise known to them as Hawkeye.

"That's the last of it." Wyatt handed him a secured cable.

"Excellent."

"I'll double check the podium area to make sure we didn't forget anything up there." Will took a step in that direction when Wyatt grabbed his arm.

"I already looked. We're good."

Brand rejoined them.

"So are we ready to head to the airport?" Liam slung his bag on his shoulder.

"No. Hawkeye wants us to stay a while longer."

Wyatt checked his watch. "We're already cutting it close on catching our flight. Don Juan and Loverboy here might be able to sweet talk the attendant at the gate into letting us board, but they can't get us through security check points with our tactical gear any quicker than necessary."

Will punched him in the arm. "I'll have you know our skills come in handy as much as your ability to deal with PTSD victims, so don't knock it."

"Let's not squabble, guys," Brand ordered. "We'll still make our flight, even if we have to get a police escort to the airport or something. Let's double check to make sure we have all of our gear secured."

Liam and the guys grumbled, but did the check anyway, knowing how Brand was a stickler about securing their equipment after what happened to him in Afghanistan. One of his team members hadn't packed the bag properly before they'd gone into theater, resulting in the teammate's death and leaving Brand injured with shrapnel in his chest too close to his pulmonary artery so he couldn't return to active duty.

Liam knew all about career ending injuries. He'd suffered a similar fate with his platoon in Helmand when an IED exploded. It had taken him months of physical rehabilitation at Walter Reed to learn to walk and do basic skills for himself again, like dressing, feeding, and bathing. But at least he had all of his limbs. His memory had been spotty at first, but in time it improved and he was finally back to normal. When he first started working with the Brotherhood, Hank had him at the Better Days Rehabilitation Ranch where he could finish recouping, but thankfully he'd moved on now and was able to go out on assignments like these.

"Hey, Don Juan," Will waved his hand in front of Liam's face. "Where'd you go there for a minute?"

Liam blinked, shaking the fog from his eyes. "What? Sorry. Did you say something?"

Wyatt laughed. "Yea, man. We were asking you if you were hungry. We were thinking if we time it right we might have time to stop and get some grub on the way to the airport."

"You know me. I can eat anytime of the day and still want more." Liam patted his lean stomach. "Hey, listen up. Here comes Brand and Hawkeye. That look on Brand's face tells me we aren't leaving here tonight."

"What?" Wyatt turned. "I think you're right, Don."

. . .

LIGHTS FLASHING AND SIRENS BLASTING, the two police SUVs charged through the night to the waterfront. They arrived on the scene within minutes, and Hawkeye led the way, stopping a few feet from where a woman argued with a detective who refused her entry into the bar.

"You don't understand! I was in there earlier with my friends. If I hadn't had to leave to catch the 'L,' I would have been with them when the shooting happened. I know they're still in there. I need to check to make sure they're okay."

Hawkeye turned to Brand. "That's Jules Gentry. One of your men needs to stay with her. As I understand it, she spotted the getaway car. I'll explain to the detective that your man is taking over."

Brand nodded.

"McLeod, she's yours. Find out what you can about what she knows and make sure no reporters get near her."

"You got it."

"Donovan, Kincaid, follow me," Brand ordered, leading them into the Pied Piper bar.

The overhead lights were at full throttle. There were tables with knocked over chairs. Pieces of shattered mirror and broken glass bottles littered the floor. For a crime scene, it was a madhouse with all the people walking through the evidence. There were officers, detectives, CSI, and the coroner on the scene doing their jobs. A gurney with a black body bag was ready for the van.

Crime scene tape cornered off detained patrons on the left side of the bar. Liam noticed right away a blonde in a leather jacket and short shorts, as well as her red-head companion in a short dress sitting beside her.

"I'll take the red-head," he said, before Brand could issue assignments.

Brand smirked. "Of course you will. Remember she's an assignment, not your date for the weekend. You will keep your libido in check, Don Juan."

"Hey now, you know I'm not really a lover boy like McLeod. The guys in my unit only nicknamed me that because it went with Donovan."

"But you do have a way with the ladies just the same," Wyatt pointed out.

He punched his friend in the arm. "You're not helping man. You're not helping."

"So do I get the blonde?" Wyatt asked.

Brand shook his head. "No. She's mine."

Hawkeye returned. "Good. I see you've found your assignments so far. The blonde is Carly Manning, the one who used the bat on the shooter. The other is Simone Reid. She had a gun pointed at her, fired, but no bullet. We're not sure if that means the gang has targeted her or not. Whoever is covering her can dig deeper from her point of view on it as well."

"Can do." Donovan nodded.

"Kincaid, I understand you're good with PTSD victims."

"That's right, Commander Burns."

"Then come with me. Special Victims was called in…"

Liam lost their conversation as he focused in on the red-head, trying to size her up, but he didn't get to far before he noticed Brand motioning for him to follow.

"Let's go talk to the girls," Brand said.

Liam walked behind him and stopped in front of the

women. Brand waited for them to acknowledge his presence, which took longer than Liam expected. Usually women took note of his pal right away.

"Can we help you?" the red-head said, when they both finally looked his way

"I'm Brand Chambers and my partner here is Liam Donovan. We'd like to speak with you both if you don't mind."

"We've already talked to the police and the detectives. How many more people do we have to talk to tonight before we can go home?" she asked.

"Moi," Donovan said. "And I can assure you if you do, I'll get you out of here and to your home as soon as I can."

"How do we know you aren't some Jo Blow who walked from off the street?"

"We're part of a new task force and have been assigned to protect you," Brand said, flashing her his Brotherhood Protectors Badge and his Chicago PD visitor's badge. Liam did the same.

The red-head nodded. "In that case. I'm Simone Reid. This is my friend Carly Manning."

"Hi." Carly looked at them with smeared mascara underneath her blue eyes. "Do you know how the gang member I hit with the bat is doing? No one will tell me anything other than he's been transported to the hospital criminal ward."

Her hands were trembling as she spoke, and she placed them on the table in front of her. Simone wrapped an arm around her and hugged her close.

"What do you need to know so we can get out of here?" Simone asked again. She didn't seem to care who they were or how they were going to get them out of the bar as long as they got home that night.

Brand stepped forward and knelt down beside Carly. "What made you use the bat?"

Her head snapped around quick. "He'd killed Phil. I'd crawled around through the entrance of the bar to see if there was a pulse and the man was threatening me with his gun. He claimed he would shoot me if I didn't get away from the body. I—I— snapped. When his back was turned I whacked him. Phil was the nicest man I had met in a long time. He'd protected me from myself when I'd had too much to drink earlier tonight. Then there was this thug. He came in and killed him for no reason. He—he was going to shoot me for no reason too. He had this hysterical laugh like a crazed animal. I'll never get that sound out of my head. What kind of a monster was he?"

A single tear ran down her cheek and Liam watched Brand wipe it away with the pad of his thumb.

"There isn't always an explanation for why people do what they do. It's getting late. Let's get you both out of here for the night. I'm sure if the police or detectives have any more questions for you, it can wait until the morning."

"Thank you," Carly said, reaching for a black bag that looked more like an overnight than a purse.

"Why don't you stay with me tonight," Simone suggested.

Carly nodded.

"Wait a minute, ladies." Liam waved his hand at them. "I'm afraid we can't let you do that. We're here to keep you both safe and the best way to do that is to keep you at two different locations."

"Wh-why do you think we need to be kept safe?" Carly asked. "Do you think the gang will try to retaliate against me because I swung that bat at the shooter?"

"We aren't sure. But you did keep him from getting away with the other two."

"As we understand it, Simone, you had a gun pointed at you. That could have been random. But what if it wasn't? Could there have been a reason this particular gang would target you?" Liam asked.

Simone's bottom lip began to tremble. She bit it and shook her head.

Liam looked at Brand and they exchanged knowing looks. There was more there than she was willing to tell either of them at the moment.

"Okay ladies. As promised you've answered our initial questions and we're going to get you out of here for the night. Is there anything you'd like to know or do before we leave here?" Liam asked.

Carly nodded. "Our friend Colleen. She went to the ladies, and we haven't seen her since. No one will tell us anything. Can you find out what happened to her? Have they made her stay in there while they clear the crime scene out here like they've made us stay on this side of the bar?"

"Possibly," Liam said. "But we'll check that out and see what we can find out for sure."

"What's her full name?" Brand asked.

"Colleen Summers. Why?" Simone asked. "She's not dead is she?"

"No. Nothing to that extreme," Liam assured as Brand left to find Hawkeye.

"Now while he's gone, do you need a glass of water or anything?"

The women shook their heads.

"We really just want to go home," Simone told him.

"Just a few more minutes. I promise. Are either of you cold? I could see about getting you a jacket or a blanket from one of the patrol cars."

Again they shook their heads. Simone looked up at him and smiled. "You're not from around here are you?"

"Why?"

"Your accent. It sounds mid-western."

"Oklahoma."

"Ok-la-ho-ma." She said it in a way that drew it out and made it sound rather sexy. He had a feeling he was in for a rough weekend with her.

Thankfully Brand returned with news of their friend.

Both Carly and Simone stood as soon as they saw him.

"What did you learn?"

"Where is Colleen?"

Their questions came at once, and he grinned at their eager faces. "I found out that the bus that was called to treat any of the patrons here tonight did take your friend to Chicago Medical Center to be checked out. She's alive so that should put your fears to rest."

The two hugged each other.

When they pulled apart they looked at one another and said in unison, "Jules!"

"She's outside. Or she was when we arrived," Liam

said. "She was trying to get in here, but the detective wouldn't let her because it was a crime scene."

"Then we need to go outside and talk to her. Let her know we're okay and what's happened to Colleen," Simone said, grabbing her purse off the table. "You want to protect me, Mr. Donovan, then let's get a move on. I want to see Jules."

"She may not be there anymore. One of our guys was assigned to her. He may have already taken her home."

"Well we won't know for sure until we get outside and find out."

The woman grabbed his hand and he could have sworn he felt a jolt of electricity ram through his body similar to the IED that had left his brain scrambled after the explosion in Helmand. For several moments his legs wouldn't work.

Simone turned and gave him a funny look. "Aren't you coming?"

"Yea. Of course." He shook the random wave of body memory away and followed her outside the Pied Piper, but as he suspected Will and her friend Jules was nowhere in sight.

"They're gone." Simone sounded so disappointed.

"You can call her tomorrow," Liam offered, leading her over to the black SUV that was waiting by the curb. "Let's get in and get you home before one of the reporters coming in our direction tries to interview you."

"You don't have to tell me twice." She climbed in the vehicle and he entered after her, closing the door before the driver sped away.

"Give the driver your address and he'll take us to your place."

"So you really are going home with me?"

"I've been assigned to protect you and I will be staying with you until I'm instructed otherwise. We've already been over this."

"Yea, I guess we have." She stared at him for a moment, moistened her lips with the tip of her tongue, and then leaned up toward the front and told the driver where to go.

Liam swallowed hard. Damn, but she was going to be a handful.

CHAPTER 3

SIMONE UNLOCKED her apartment and let Liam go inside first to check it out. She rolled her eyes because she didn't see how anyone knew where she lived or could have gotten inside if she'd just unlocked the door, but she allowed Mr. Macho Marine guy his due to check out her place before she went inside.

"You want anything to drink? Water? Coffee?" She asked, going to the kitchen and getting herself a bottle of water.

"I know it's late. Really too late to eat, but we skipped dinner thinking we would grab something on our way to the airport. But that didn't happen when we were called to duty. Could I maybe grab a sandwich or something?" Liam asked.

Simone grinned. "Sure. Let's see what I've got that's edible." She opened up the refrigerator door again and looked inside. "I've been out of town this week on business. Just got back and haven't been to the store yet."

"You got peanut butter?" he asked.

"That I have." She pulled the half loaf of bread from the shelf and closed the door. "Do you like your bread toasted?"

"Sure."

She put the bread in the toaster and then opened up the cabinet, taking out the jar of peanut butter. Then she got a small plate down as well as a knife from the drawer.

After making his sandwich she showed him where everything that he might need to know was located in the kitchen while he ate. Then she took him to the spare bedroom where he'd be sleeping.

"The bedrooms use the same bathroom. It's a Jack and Jill set up so be sure when you are in here you lock both doors so I don't walk in on you and I'll do the same so you don't walk in on me."

"Got it."

"Okay. Good night then."

Simone went into her room, shut the door and went straight to the bathroom to clean up from where she'd showered before leaving to go out earlier. She didn't want Liam to think she was a slob. Not that she cared what he thought at the moment. Locking the door, she stripped off and showered again, trying to remove all memory from the night's events, but it did little good. She couldn't forget the silver .45 pointed at her face or the gang member's laughed.

She sucked her bottom lip between her teeth, and began breathing faster and faster at the thought of a bullet really coming out of that gun. She'd be dead right now. She'd known it then, but she hadn't allowed herself the luxury to dwell upon it. Pushing the water off, she sank to the shower floor, pulled her knees up to her chest and hugged herself close. Laying her head against her knees, the flood gates opened as her anguish and fear released itself with the tears she'd kept bottled up inside.

LIAM SETTLED in the spare room and tried to get comfortable on the bed. He always had a hard time adjusting to a new bed, no matter where he was sleeping. He had just closed his eyes, when he thought he heard muffled crying. His eyes flashed open and he sat up. He turned his head and listened closely. Was it coming from somewhere in the apartment?

Reaching for his pants, he put them on again. He stood and listened a few more seconds, hoping he could dismiss the sound as a cat in another apartment, but it didn't stop. It definitely was a woman crying.

He went to the closed bathroom door, tried the knob and found it locked. "Simone, are you in there?"

There was no response, but the crying continued. He pressed his ear to the door and the sobs grew louder. They were definitely coming from the other side. It was Simone, whether she had answered him or not. The woman he had met at the bar tonight hadn't come across as the crying in the shower type, but something now sure had her spooked. And why wouldn't it? She'd had a gun pointed at her and the trigger pulled. Maybe her fate had finally flashed before her eyes.

He had to get to her, but breaking down the door wasn't the answer. She wouldn't appreciate that. And he was certain Hawkeye wouldn't either, when the bill to replace the door was delivered to Chicago PD. He thought for a moment. She'd said the bathrooms were Jack and Jill and there was another entrance in her bedroom. That would mean going into her private sanctuary to get to her, and, having two younger sisters, he knew how their rooms were off limits. But he'd take any flack she gave him tomorrow for intruding into her territory.

He left his bedroom and walked the short distance to her door and, turned the knob, thankful she hadn't locked it as well. A bedside lamp burned low and he noticed the room was similar to his, except it was decorated in a different style bed and comforter. She had taste like his sister Janine. Spotting the bathroom door, he went to it and opened it.

The crying sobs greeted him loudly.

"Simone, are you okay?"

A frosted shower curtain blocked his view of her, and all he could see was a shadowy image huddled on the floor of the shower. The crying ceased. He heard labored breathing and sniffling before she finally responded to his question.

"N-no."

"Are you hurt?"

"N-no."

"Care to talk about it?"

"You wouldn't understand."

"Wouldn't I?" He saw a slender door in the bathroom and opened it up to find stacks of towels and wash clothes. He pulled out what looked to be the largest towel, one they called a bath sheet. His mom had some of those, and were his favorites. He pushed it through the edge of the shower curtain toward her. "Did you forget I'm here to protect you? I've been in combat before. I've been if Afghanistan. Helmand to be exact. That is where I was injured and got discharged from my duties as a Marine. So I think I'd understand about anything you could tell me, Sweetheart."

"I'm not your sweetheart."

"That's a girl. Your fight's back all ready. You're sounding more like the feisty red head I met tonight at the bar. I'm going to step out of here now and let you get dressed. I'll be waiting in the kitchen if you want to talk. Do you need water or a drink of some kind to help you sleep?

"Water will be fine."

He went to the kitchen and opened the refrigerator taking out two bottles of water, then sat down at the table, waiting for her to join him. PTSD wasn't his forte like it was Wyatt's, but he'd had his share of therapy sessions during recovery at Walter Reed, working through the feeling of surviving the ordeal. He was certain he could get her at least talking about what happened tonight and listen if nothing else. Sometimes that was all a person needed was someone to listen to what they were feeling.

It wasn't long before she opened her bedroom door and came out in pajamas and a robe. Her hair was damp, but combed straight, totally different than it had looked at the bar earlier. She sat stiffly in the chair across from him and stared blankly. He slid her a bottle of water.

"You have tattoos," she said.

"Just a few."

"I thought about getting one once, but I couldn't make up my mind what to get, so I didn't."

"They're not for everyone."

She unscrewed the cap off the water and took a long drink. "You'd never get Carly to do it."

"Why is that?"

"Too timid, uptight. Her ex-husband had her under his thumb for too long. Before that, her parents."

"It really doesn't matter what she'd do. It matters what you'd do, if you wanted one, that is. Do you want one?"

She nodded. "I might get one. Someday."

"Survivor. A simple word tattooed on the underside of your wrist. A reminder that you overcame tonight's event."

She took another long drink of water. "*That.* I don't know why that gun was pointed at me. Why would someone do that? Point a gun at another person and pull the trigger, then laugh like a crazed person when there was a shot fired and no bullet?"

"It bothered you that he laughed."

"Hell yes."

"It would have bothered me too. I'd have beaten the SOB if he'd done it to me."

"Carly did. With the bat. Not sure he was the same one, but she got one of them. She got Phil's shooter. While the other two ran away."

Liam nodded watching her drain the last of the water before she squashed the bottle with her hands.

"Do you think you will be able to sleep tonight?" he asked.

"I don't know. I'm so agitated right now. I want to cry. I want to scream. I want to hit something."

He stood up and walked to her, held out his hand for her to take. "Stand up."

"What?" She jerked her head up in his direction.

"I want you to hit me. Hit me with all your might. You won't hurt me. I'm solid as a rock. Kick, scream, cry, hit. Get it out."

Simone stood and did what he asked unsure that he knew what he was doing, but she did it. She threw a few punches. A right. A left.

Liam shook his head.

"No. No. Stop." He grabbed her fist and held it. "You aren't putting your anger into it. Try it again. This time imagine I'm the gang member who pointed that gun at you. I have pulled that trigger, and I've laughed my ass off at you. Release that anger on me."

She swallowed, thinking about how that gunman had made her feel. She screamed and she kicked his shins with her bare feet and she hit at him with her fists, pounding against his perfectly, rounded pecks. Beating on his tattoo that said *One life, One Chance* until the skin around it was red because this was her chance to take back control. She cried, lashing out at him over and over until her body was spent and all she could do was fall against him. His wonderfully large arms wrapped around her, holding her exhausted body against him.

"Feel better?" he finally asked, breaking the silence.

"Yes. Surprisingly enough, I do."

"Can you sleep now?"

"I think so."

"Perfect." He scooped her up in his arms and carried her from the kitchen area to her bedroom and sat her down at the foot of her bed. "Goodnight, Simone. I'm on the other side of your bathroom if you need me."

"Goodnight, Mr. Donovan."

"Liam will do. Or Don Juan as my buddies call me."

She grinned. "Don Juan? Should I be worried having you in my apartment?"

"No Ma'am. Not at all." He left her, closing her door behind him.

THE NEXT MORNING Simone was up early making out her shopping lists for the different errands that needed to be run that day. She had recon work to do on her failed business trip and she couldn't work with her protector in the apartment reminding her of what happened last night. She knew that. Getting out her pent-up frustration had helped her sleep like a baby, but as soon as she got up and heard him in the shower this morning, she'd been on edge all over again because of what his being here meant. She didn't need him around every minute of the day reminding her of that gun pointed in her face. Not when she had to figure out what she was going to tell her boss on Monday about her not so stellar business trip with Webster-Reynolds.

She heard the bedroom door open and footsteps coming down the hallway before he arrived. "There's coffee if you care for a cup."

"Thanks. I don't mind if I do."

"I hope you slept well. The guest room is rarely used.

Only when my mom and step-dad come to town for a visit."

He nodded and picked up the non-dairy creamer, adding some to his cup as well as sugar, then stirring before coming over to the table where she sat. "What's that?"

"Shopping lists. I have each store and address at the top, if you don't mind? Unless I can go with you?"

"No. I'll take care of it alone. You should stay here out of sight until Chicago PD has a better handle on what went down last night. I know Hawkeye was hoping to get a lead on the two gang members that got away. Until that happens you are a moving target."

"Gee, thanks. That right there makes me feel one hundred times better. Not only did I have a .45 pointed in my face, but now you tell me I'm a moving target."

"Figure of speech, but yeah, it pretty much sums it up. As long as you stay in your apartment or have me with you when you go out, then you should be safe."

"But you don't know that for sure."

"No. I don't. But I am here to protect you."

Simone reached for her purse and pulled out what cash she had. I think this will cover it. If not, here is a credit card. The pharmacy has my card on file and can do express pay."

"Got it. I'll be back as soon as I can then."

"Take your time. I'm going to do some work for a client for Monday. I'll see you when you return."

CHAPTER 4

LIAM WAS HALFWAY through the shopping list Simone had given him when he felt his phone buzz in his pocket. He pulled his shopping cart over in the aisle and looked to see who was trying to reach him. It was Brand wanting a status update.

He quickly typed his response.

"Help! I'm being domesticated. She's got me doing her grocery shopping! "

"Hey man. You wanted the redhead. Suck it up. Otherwise everything okay on your end?"

"Yeah. Sweet pad. Got my own room. What about you?"

"Sofa sleeper."

"Better than the floor."

"Do me a favor. Find out about Carly's ex-husband. I think he's keeping tabs on her. I need to know what I'm dealing with over here."

"Will do. Over and out."

Carly's ex-husband. Simone had mentioned him last

night. What had she said about him? Liam thought for a moment. Oh yeah. They'd been talking about tattoos. Simone had said Carly was too uptight to get one. That it had much to do with her ex-husband keeping her under his thumb and that her parents were much the same. Maybe Brand needed to know that.

He typed the message, but didn't hit send. He debated about whether that info was hearsay or fact as he continued on down the aisle looking for the next item on the list. He hesitated for quite a while as he shopped trying to make up his mind if it was something Brand needed to know or not. In the end as he finished the list at the first store, he decided to delete the text and hoped he'd made the right choice.

SIMONE REFILLED her coffee cup and was headed back to her desk to work when her cellphone rang. She grabbed it, saw it was Carly and instead, headed for the living room.

"Hey, good to hear your voice, are you alone?" Simone curled up in the oversized armchair in her living room.

"Yes. Are you?" Carly said on the other end of the line.

"I am. Sent my guy out shopping. What did you do?"

"Same. Or rather, he insisted. The reason I called, I got word on Colleen. She's still at the hospital. Brand said it was because she was resting last night, but I have a funny feeling something more is going on than he is telling me. He also said she's awake and that the doctor was checking her out, and that her parents are there arguing on which one is going to take her home. That makes me believe something happened last night we don't know about, otherwise why would they be arguing over her going home with one of them?"

"You always have a sixth sense, Carly, except when it came to Justin Porter. If you have a feeling something isn't right with Colleen I believe you. We should go to the hospital and see her."

"I don't know. It's too risky. I believe what Brand said about our lives being in danger."

"Are you sure you can trust him completely? Especially if he is keeping secrets about Colleen from us."

"Maybe he is telling me all he can, when he can. Besides, he found a man watching my place last night. The man was still here this morning and Brand found out the guy works for Justin Porter."

Simone thought about that for a quick second, her mind working overtime. She pulled up the Uber app on her phone and punched in her ride request. "I'm coming over. You don't need to be left alone if that slime ball Porter has a man following you."

"What about your safety, Simone?" Carly asked. "I don't want you putting your life in jeopardy on my account. You've already had a gun pointed at you and the trigger pulled."

"Don't you worry your pretty little head over that. Donnie and I had a long discussion about it this morning and we agree it was a fluke."

"Donnie?"

"Donovan. My guy. He said he got the nickname Don Juan from his Marine buddies, but until I see him put the moves on me and earn those stripes I'm going to refer to him as Donnie."

"Simone, be real. He's not going to put the moves on you. He's here to protect you. Not seduce you."

"No man alive can resist me when I make a play for him. Just you watch. I'll have little Donnie in my hands before the weeks out."

"Little Donnie. I don't even want to know what you mean by that."

"You already do, Carly." Simone rolled her eyes at her friend. "So tell me, when are you going to put my hand-cuffs to work?"

"None of your business. I don't kiss and tell."

"Isn't that the truth? You're no fun in the bedroom." She took a breath hoping her bravado kept the truth from her friend. She'd had to talk fast to keep her mind off that gun when Carly brought it up. "I've just got confirmation from my Uber on pickup. I'll be there soon and I'll call when I'm outside your building."

"You really shouldn't be doing this."

"Be ready when I get there. We're going to see Colleen."

Simone ended the call, knowing that if she didn't give Carly time to protest that her friend had no other choice than to go along with her on this. Bravado or not, it would give her and Liam good fodder for an argument that could lead to excellent foreplay. She'd had some of the best sex after a heated fight with a lover. Not that Liam would necessarily go along with that plan, but the idea of sex right now to get her mind off of that gun and bullet sounded like the thing to get lost in.

. . .

THEY GOT out of the Uber at the entrance to Chicago Med and went inside to the information desk. They typed in Colleen's name at the kiosk to find out what floor she was on before heading to the bank of elevators.

Once inside the elevator, Carly turned to Simone. "I still think this was a bad idea."

"You didn't have to come with me," Simone pointed out. "You could have stayed at your apartment doing your laundry."

"No I couldn't. I would have worried something would have happened to you alone. The smart thing was for you to stay at your place until Donovan returned."

"Live a little, Carly. Take chances."

The elevator dinged, signaling they'd arrived to their floor before the doors opened and the girls stepped out. All discussion about what was right or wrong ceased as they following the corridor signs down the hallway to where Colleen's room was located.

The sound of arguing voices wafted down the hall and the two looked at one another.

"Geeze, I hope they aren't in her room doing that."

"Mr. and Mrs. Summers never had tact when it came to disagreeing," Simone said.

Someone made a sharp pitched whistle sound cutting them off. "Enough. I know you want what's best for your daughter, but this isn't it." A door shut, preventing Simone and Carly from overhearing whatever else was being said on the matter.

"I wonder if that was Colleen's guy," Carly said.

"Maybe. We better hurry and find her while he's preoccupied with mom and dad or we're busted."

"Oh, *now* you think of that."

Simone rolled her eyes and grabbed Carly's arm dragging her with her down the hall toward the nurses' station.

Colleen's room was directly across the hall from the station, which was good. They went inside and slid the curtain back so no one would see them visiting with her.

"Oh my God," Simone gasped when she saw the bruising and swelling on Colleen's face.

"She must have been attacked in the bathroom. That's the reason she was in there so long," Carly said. "And you wanted to leave when those guys came in."

"I-I had no idea. The three of us had been to that bar so many times before. It was always a safe place to go until last night. Do you think she was raped?" Simone whispered.

Carly moved to the opposite side of the bed and reached for Colleen's hand that didn't have an IV sticking in it.

Their friend flinched at her touch. Her eyes fluttered open and her lips began to tremble once she focused. Tears began to roll down her cheeks.

"Sh-h-h, don't cry. It's okay. You're okay. You're safe." Carly patted her hand.

Simone stepped forward and brushed hair away from Colleen's forehead. "We're here for you."

"What happened to me?" Colleen asked.

"You don't know?"

Colleen shook her head.

Carly looked at Simone, then back down at Colleen. "Honey, we don't know. Do you remember going out with us last night?"

"Yes. I remember dancing with you guys, but that's it."

"We were getting ready to leave, but you had to go to the restroom," Simone said. "So you went alone."

"We waited for you out front, at the bar, but then the bar got robbed. The bartender was shot and we were lucky to have gotten out alive. In all the chaos, we never knew what happened to you. We found out you were taken to the hospital last night to be checked out."

"Your parents are here, down the hall arguing about whose going to take you home. Have you seen them yet?" Simone asked.

Colleen groaned. "Carly, I know I made fun of your apartment last night, but let me go home with you."

They laughed.

"Hey, you are remembering something from last night. That is good." Carly smiled at her. "What did the doctor say when he saw you this morning?"

"That I needed to rest and stay here another day because of my memory loss and some tests they want to run on me."

"Did they examine you?" Simone asked.

Colleen nodded. "*That* didn't happen. But for what did, I still feel violated. I don't remember it, but he did something to me. I feel icky and I want to shower a dozen times. I know I never want to wear that skirt again."

The curtain scrapped back fast and a young, blond man wearing tactical gear came into the room. Simone guessed this was Wyatt.

"Ladies, I don't assume you were given permission to be here?"

"Are you going to do something about it?" She asked, walking toward him. She came nose to nose with him, hoping to intimidate him.

The guy didn't flinch. He slid the glass room door shut, pulled out his phone and punched in a number. Then he put the phone up to his ear. "Don Juan, I think you've lost something very important and you need to come collect it now before I report you to Brand for slacking on your duties. It has red-hair and curvaceous ..."

Wyatt laughed into the phone. "See you then."

"Who's he?" Colleen asked.

"He's been assigned to protect you," Carly explained. "We've all got a guy assigned to protect us after what happened last night at the bar."

"Really? Why?"

"The bar shooting was gang related. Simone and I are witnesses inside. Jules saw the getaway car outside because she came back when she heard the gunshots."

"I heard them too."

"You did?"

Colleen nodded, closing her eyes. "That's what caused my attacker to run away."

Wyatt came over to the bed. "Did she say what I think she said?"

Carly nodded.

"Colleen, what else do you remember from last night?" he asked.

"I'm tired. I need to rest now."

Wyatt punched in a few more numbers on his phone and walked back toward the sliding doors. "Brand, Wyatt here. You need to come to Chicago Med. There's been a development. Sure. Just get here as fast as you can. Thanks."

He turned around and looked at them. "Ladies, you might as well take a seat and get comfortable. You're gonna be here a while. And then you won't be able to sit without remembering the chewing out you get."

CHAPTER 5

LIAM WAS ALMOST at Simone's apartment when he got Wyatt's call so he hurried to drop off the groceries before going to Chicago Med. He should have known she'd not have stayed put while he was gone. She'd made out such a long list of errands for him to run, it should have been a clear sign there was something up. But she'd played it so cool with him this morning, even telling him to take his time since she was going to be catching up on work for Monday. He had to hand it to her. She'd fooled him once, but she wouldn't do it again.

He took the "L" to the hospital expecting to get there in a straight shot, but the many stops along the way added time he hadn't anticipated, which had him sweating it by the time he reached the hospital. Then he had to figure out how to get to the information desk and locate which floor Colleen was on. He got off on the wrong floor and took the wrong corridor, but then he found a bank of elevators and got back on to head up to the right floor once again.

When he stepped off he was near the nurses' station and came face to face with Brand and Commander Burns. Shit!

"Wyatt called you both in about this? I swear I only left Simone alone to go get a few groceries and some things she demanded she had to have. I never imagined she'd leave her apartment."

"So it happened to both of you?" Burns asked.

Brand grimaced.

"Both of us?" Donovan looked at Brand.

"Yeah, both Carly and Simone are here visiting Colleen. I guess Wyatt didn't tell you that?"

"No. He just told me I lost something and if I didn't want him telling you, I'd better get here fast."

Hawkeye chuckled.

"This isn't funny," Brand grumbled.

"Not at all," Donovan agreed.

"I beg to differ. Two females giving highly trained military operatives the slip? You can fight for this country, and are trained to serve and protect, yet you can't keep them in their apartments? This isn't going to look good when I try to get funding to get a program going here in Chicago if you can't even keep these two safe."

"It won't happen again," Brand assured him.

"It better not. I'm counting on all four of you to do your jobs and make my task easy. I want this program for my city."

"We understand," Brand said. "Don't we, Donovan?"

"Yes, Sir. We have your six on this."

The sliding glass door to a room across from the nurses' station opened and Wyatt came out, closing the door back. "I thought I heard voices. Before you go in there chewing the girls out, their visit has been good for Colleen. She's been responsive, and remembering things about last night with them that my questioning couldn't get her to recall. I know they disobeyed and risked their lives coming here, but it has been good in the end. I still would bring the wrath of God down on them, but keep in mind what was accomplished just the same."

"Did she get a good look at her attacker? Should we bring down a sketch artist?" Hawkeye asked.

"She hasn't proclaimed that yet, but she did say she heard the gunshots and that is why her attacker ran off. She napped and when she woke up she talked about him taking her purse, and how she was worried about her apartment and being robbed and her credit cards being maxed out. That's the reason I contacted your office, Commander."

"I was in the area so I dropped by to see how things were going."

"How did her parents take the news she wasn't going home with them?" Brand asked.

"Not well, but when I explained she wasn't going to her apartment, but a safe house and why, they agreed that was the best plan because of their work obligations. In return, I promised to keep them well aware of what was going on with her."

"That was handled well, Kincaid." Hawkeye stepped forward and touched him on the shoulder. "Let's go in and meet this courageous young woman and her daring friends, under better circumstances."

Liam didn't like this. He didn't care if the commander

thought this was under better circumstances. Simone had just made a fool out of him and she'd regret it. He didn't care if her visit had been a help to Colleen or not. He glanced at her sitting with Carly across the room, looking all smug, eyeing him like he was a piece of candy. That was a change in attitude since this morning. He didn't like the way her looking at him like that made him feel as if she were undressing him with her eyes. He was supposed to be the Don Juan in the relationship, not her.

Colleen turned her head toward the doorway.

"This is Commander Burns from Chicago PD, Brand Chambers and Liam Donovan," Wyatt explained. "They are here to check in on how things are going and to collect Simone and Carly."

"What if we don't want to go?" Simone asked.

"You will do what you're told young woman or I'll have you taken down to central booking," Hawkeye told her.

"On what charges?"

Liam wanted to slap his hand over her mouth and shut her up, but she'd probably bite him. Maybe he could find something to gag her with before she made matters worse. Didn't she know you didn't talk to a commander that way?

"Impeding an investigation."

"And how would I be doing that?"

"By causing more work for your protector and the police to make sure you're safe, when my officers need to be out in the field looking for your friend's attacker and the gang members who tried to rob the Pied Piper. I'm sure I could come up with other charges to keep you in a holding cell until we find the perps. *Or* you can go back to your apartment with Mr. Donovan and stay in comfort."

"I do have to go back to work Monday."

"Then he'll go with you. I'll send a driver and a car around for your use."

"I have a job interview next week. I need this job to pay my bills. Please, can I keep the interview?" Carly asked.

"No. Not after this stunt," Brand barked.

"Brand, take it down a notch." Hawkeye arched a brow at him, before turning toward Carly. "I don't see why that should be a problem if Brand goes with you. We want you to carry on your normal routine as much as possible. You aren't a prisoner by any means. However, we do want to keep you both safe and measures must be taken to ensure that, so if it feels like your wings of freedom have been clipped temporarily, that's all it is – temporary."

"Thank you, Commander." Carly paused. "There is one more thing. I'd like to be able to go to the bartender's funeral, whenever that is, to pay my respects to his wife, if possible. Can that be arranged?"

The Commander was hesitant for a moment, but he finally nodded. "That can happen, Ms. Manning. I'm sure his wife will appreciate that."

After a few moments Simone leaned toward Carly. "Geeze your guy is a hard ass."

"He's tough, but fair."

"You're not defending him are you?"

Carly half-shrugged. "I get him."

"You and the men you pick."

"I haven't picked him."

Simone tilted her head and looked at her pointedly. "If you say so."

Carly shook her head and went back over to hold Colleen's hand while the commander asked her a few questions. Simone decided to follow. She didn't want to be left out on whatever Colleen was saying.

"I-I'm not sure what he looked like. He came through the door so fast and hit me in the face with his hand. I-I don't think I'd be any help for a sketch artist."

"You may think that now, but I'd like you to try. We can bring in a behavioral scientist who can take you on a journey through a series of questions. The results will help you reveal more than you ever imagined you'd remember."

"Like a profiler?" Colleen asked. "Something like they do on *Criminal Minds?*"

The commander nodded. "But this method is real."

"How soon can you have someone here?" Wyatt asked.

"I can arrange to get someone here as early as this afternoon. The sooner we can get a sketch of her attacker, the better we'll be able to find him."

"When do you think Colleen will be released from the hospital?" Carly asked.

"That is up to the doctor," Wyatt said. "He wasn't hopeful this morning but that was because he wanted to run tests."

"So her staying here has nothing to do with trying to keep her in a safe location?" Carly questioned.

"If that was what we were going for, we'd have to have a guard posted outside her door to track who comes in and out of this room. A hospital is too public to be safe."

The commander turned to Brand. "My car and driver are downstairs. You and Donovan can escort the women to their respective apartments for now. I'll order a car detail for you both to have at your disposal. All you have to do is call when you want it. I'll send both of you the information."

"Thanks, Hawkeye." Brand motioned to Carly. "Say your good-byes so we can head out."

She nodded and looked down at Colleen, giving her hand a squeeze. "I'll see you soon. I know you're in good hands with Wyatt. You can call me if you want to talk."

"Good luck on your interview."

"Thanks. I'll need it." Carly stepped away from the bed and turned toward Simone. "Let's go girl."

"You're going to let him order you around like that?" Simone questioned.

"He's not ordering me around. It's time to go. Colleen needs to rest. Can't you see how tired she looks?"

"Simone!" Donovan said, his tone full of irritation.

"Yes, Donnie?" Simone allowed the words to purr from her mouth for effect.

Brand grunted. "Donnie?"

Simone sidled up to Carly and whispered in her ear. "I got him right where I want him. Before the week's out. I tell you, before the week is out."

Carly rolled her eyes and tried to stifle a laugh.

CHAPTER 6

"WHAT THE HELL, SIMONE?" Liam asked as soon as they got back to her apartment. He was so frustrated at her he couldn't stand still, so he paced in front of her as he talked. "What's with this Donnie crap? I told you my name is Liam or you could call me Don Juan like my pals do. Nothing was said about Donnie? And why were you looking at me from across the room like I'm man candy? And purring my name like you're a cat? Was that all show for your friend? Like you're going to get me in your bed or something, because let me tell you right now, sweetheart. That's not going to happen."

"I told you before, I'm not your sweetheart. It was an act, okay? Carly brought up the gun and the bullet and I went into auto mode talking cheeky about you. Like I wanted to get you into bed to take the focus off of the shooting and what happened at the bar. That's me. The free-spirit. The pole dancer when we go out to bars. The attention seeker." She sucked in her breath and ran her fingers through her hair. "I had to take my mind off of anything about last night and put it on you."

He planted his hands on his hips and fixed a glare at her, finally calm enough to stand still. "And the way you were talking back to Commander Burns. That was disrespectful. You can't blame your behavior on anyone or anything but yourself. That man is the reason you have me here protecting you. And speaking of which, what gave you the idea that you could call up an Uber and go to that hospital with Carly in the first place?"

She blanched. "Not the brightest idea I've had. Carly tried to talk me out of it, but when I found out Colleen was there and Brand was possibly keeping info about her away from us, I had to go."

"He wasn't."

"I know that now, but at the time, I didn't."

"You've got to learn to trust us. Me, Brand, Wyatt, and Will. The four of us will do everything in our power to keep you and your girlfriends safe. That is our job. Do you understand that?"

Simone nodded, slowly sinking in the oversized armchair in her living room.

"Good. Is there a workout room in the apartment building?"

"No. Why?"

"I was curious. Some apartment complexes have them. I thought yours might. I need to work off my anger right now. What about the roof?"

"I've never been up there."

"Okay. Go change into workout gear. We're going down to Chicago PD. There's a gym at the station. You can either join me or look the part whichever you prefer."

"I don't see why I can't just stay at home," she said.

"Because we tried that before and it didn't work. You broke that trust already."

He saw her roll her eyes before she went into her room.

"You're making me feel like a child."

"When you act like one then you deserve the repercussions."

Simone slammed her bedroom door. And she'd thought Brand was a hard ass. Don Juan was no light weight either. But she had to admit she deserved it. She'd left the apartment even though he'd trusted her to stay put while he was gone. Carly tried to tell her to stay home, but she wouldn't listen. She never listened. She was too much like her father on that account. Wasn't that what her mother always said?

Simone sighed, opened up her dresser and pulled out her workout clothes.

What was done was done. She wasn't going to regret it for one moment now. She'd seen Colleen. She'd found out what had happened to her friend. No harm had come to them. So what was the big deal?

If she'd been shot while she was gone, that would have been on her, right?

Wrong.

The blame would have landed on Liam's shoulders for not keeping her safe. He'd left her alone in her apartment while going out to do the shopping when he should have called in back up to watch her apartment while he stepped out. He'd trusted her to stay put. And she'd broken it. Now he wouldn't let her out of his sight.

"Stupid, Simone. Really stupid move," she grumbled, changing into her yoga pants and tank. She slipped on a zippered hoody, pulled her hair back into a ponytail and put on her socks and tennis shoes before going back into the living room.

"I called for a driver. He should be here in ten."

"I'm sorry, Liam. I didn't think about the position I was putting you in when I left the apartment. I wasn't just risking my life, I was putting your career on the line."

He looked at her for a moment, and then nodded. "I appreciate you saying it, Simone. Just remember that before you make a rash decision again. Ask yourself first how this will affect me and others. We still don't know why that gang member singled you out at the bar and pulled the trigger. Did he know the chamber was empty when he did? Was that why he laughed when he saw the horror on your face? Did he do it to get a rush?"

Simone nodded, moisture pooling at the corner of her eyes with him talking about the incident. Her mind immediately went to her dad missing for some reason and how he'd react if something were to happen to her. Likewise, how would her mom and her stepdad, Leland handle the news as well. She hadn't even thought to give them a call and tell them what had happened to her, and didn't know if she should because that would only alarm and worry them for nothing. But in the same instance, she didn't want either to be upset with her for not telling them, especially if something more serious were to happen later. What if the bar shooting had made the national news?

"You got quiet. What's running through that head of yours?"

"Whether I should call my mom in Florida and tell her about the incident in the bar or not. I have a relationship with my family, unlike Carly."

"Then I think you should."

"Yeah. I'll do that tonight." She followed him toward the door. "I'll also tell her about my dad missing."

"Your father is missing? Wouldn't she know that?"

"They're divorced. She's remarried."

"How do you know he's missing?"

"Because his coworkers haven't heard from him in three weeks. I went looking for him last week when I was on a business trip to DC where he was reported to have been before his business partners lost touch. But I had no luck finding him. I'm worried something is wrong."

Liam turned and looked at her. "Simone, why didn't you tell me about this before?"

"Why? What does my dad being missing have to do with anything that is going on?"

"Probably nothing. But that explains the vibe I got from you in the bar last night that you weren't telling me everything when you bit your lip."

"You sensed that?"

"Yeah, I did. Brand did too."

She smiled at him. "Carly always says that a tell-tale sign that I'm lying."

"She must know you well."

"We were sorority sisters in college. We've been very close ever since."

"Still, does your dad up and go missing a lot? Is this typical behavior for him?"

"Sometimes. His business partners aren't worried because they say he's usually working on a new lead for a client, but no one goes incommunicado for three weeks."

"What kind of work does he do?"

"Sales. Some big name contracts. He's mentioned having a few government contracts in the past."

"Is that all you know?"

"Pretty much. He changes divisions within his company every few years, so I can't keep up with what line of clientele he is working. He's happy and that is all that matters. I see him more now than I did as a kid really, so that makes me happy."

"You don't think he's into anything shady, do you?"

"My dad?" Simone asked, shaking her head. "Never."

Liam nodded, crossing his arms over his chest as they waited in the lobby of the apartment building for the driver to arrive. When he pulled up, Liam ushered her quickly into the black SUV.

The workout room at Chicago PD was nice and she used the treadmill, the elliptical, and did about a hundred spins on the bike while Liam used the punching bag and lifted weights. The whole time she worked out, her mind was on what Liam asked about her dad. *You don't think he's into anything shady, do you?* What would give him that idea from what she had said?

An hour and a half later, they were headed back to her apartment. He had the driver stop by a street fair on the way back and they sampled a few of the food trucks before they finally made it back to her place. She was amazed at the amount of food Liam could put away for someone so fit and muscular.

"I'm going to go shower and then call my mom," Simone said, as soon as she opened the door. "I'll let you know when the bathroom is free so you can use it."

"Sure, take your time."

LIAM HEADED to the guest room, kicked off his shoes and sat down on the edge of the bed to text Brand. He'd been thinking about that text he opted not to send that morning about Carly. After his conversation with Simone this afternoon, he decided maybe he should share the fact that Carly's ex-husband and parents were over-bearing with Brand after all. He also wanted to let Brand know there might be something up with Simone's father. That was definitely something he was going to be looking into. If the man was really missing, he needed to be found, connected to the bar shooting or not. He could tell that Simone was worried, whether she admitted it or not.

In fact, he was pretty sure that Simone's brashness was all an act. She'd admitted as much to him when they returned from the hospital. The only thing he couldn't understand was why? Why did she feel she needed to act that way? Was it for attention growing up? Had her parents fought often before their divorce and that was a way for her to gain their attention? Or had it been an attempt to get her father's attention? She'd also said she spends more time with him now that she did when she was growing up.

He had to admit one thing, Simone Reid was one complex woman to figure out. She was more than the feisty red head he'd first seen in the aftermath of the Pied Piper Bar shooting. She was vulnerable, and if you were able to get past her smart mouthed exterior, there was a softness, he was sure of it.

CHAPTER 7

"You've got to be kidding me!" Simone screamed at her phone, half-awake, as she reached for it to turn off whatever was making it explode with beeping and singing at the same time.

Her bedroom door burst open, banging against the wall, and Liam was in her room with his gun drawn, but pointed toward the ceiling.

"Holy crap!" She sat up quickly, forgetting about her squawking phone. She pulled the sheet up around her with one hand and grabbed the phone with the other, shutting the noise off. She laid down the phone and with both index fingers pointed toward her door. "Get out! Get out!"

"I heard screams."

"That was me yelling at my phone." She unlocked her screen and viewed the text message from her boss, Robert Cranston. He wanted her to come into the office immediately that morning, even though it was Sunday. "Jiminy, this can't be good."

"What?" Liam asked, ignoring her order to leave the room.

"I've been summoned into work by my boss. Can you call for a car? Unless you want to risk taking a taxi?"

"I'll call for a car while you dress. Do you know what this is about?"

"Oh yeah. I know, and frankly I'm surprised he didn't call me yesterday."

Liam's right brow arched and he cocked his head to the side.

"Don't look at me that way. I told you I spent time on my last business trip trying to find my dad. What I didn't tell you is I spent more time on that than on my client."

"I see."

She shrugged.

"So this thing with your dad could be more serious than you first let on."

Simone sucked in a breath and nodded. "Yes. Now get out of my room so I can get dressed."

As soon as the door shut behind Liam, Simone was out of bed and in front of her closet doors, opening them wide, stepping inside to decide what she should wear for a royal chewing out. She decided to wear her favorite pantsuit that made her look like she'd stepped out of a store on Rodeo Drive. She paired it with sedate leather pumps and a matching purse. An up-do and teardrop pearl earrings finished off the look.

Liam had mixed up a box of muffins in the time it took her to get ready as well as made coffee for her."

"Our ride will be here in ten. You've got time to eat something and have a coffee," he explained.

She smiled. "Thanks. I might get used to you being around if you fix me breakfast every morning."

He chuckled. "I like to eat and breakfast is the most important meal of the day."

"You sound like my mom." She drank from her cup, welcoming the soothing effect of the java and caffeine.

"My mom, you mean." He refilled her coffee cup. "She was big on starting each day with something in your stomach, even if it was a piece of dry toast as you ran out the door for the bus."

Simone grinned. "I think I'd like her."

"She'd like you too."

"Would she?" Simone cocked her head to the side.

"My mom likes everyone until they give her a reason otherwise." He turned away and washed up the muffin pan, dried and put it away.

When she brought over her empty coffee mug, she noticed he'd already washed the mixing bowl as well. Everything was neat and tidy before they left, and she was certain that if she went to his bedroom that she'd find the bed was made without a crease in the covers.

WHEN THEY ARRIVED at her office building, she swiped them in with her badge and was greeted by a security guard who escorted them to the elevator, unlocking it for them to go up to the appropriate floor. Her boss was waiting for her, so that meant the security guard must have been instructed to radio up that she was on her way.

"Who's this with you, Simone?" Mr. Cranston asked.

"Liam Donovan, my bodyguard. I don't suppose you heard about the Pied Piper shooting Friday night?"

"I did hear about that. It made the front page of the Saturday morning paper and was on the local news. Were you involved?"

"A witness, sir. And Mr. Donovan has been assigned to keep me safe until I can testify at trial."

"I see. But you are free to leave the city? Even the state if necessary?"

"Of course, sir. As long as I inform Chicago PD of my whereabouts. Isn't that right, Liam?" She turned to him.

"That's right."

"Very well. Can we speak privately in my office? Or will Mr. Donovan need to check it out first to make sure I'm not luring you in there on false pretenses? Or that I plan you harm?" Mr. Cranston said.

Simone glanced at Liam and saw his jaw muscle twitch.

"I wasn't planning to, Mr. Cranston, but since you brought it up, I think I will check your office out. Never can be too safe in these situations."

"Liam, please, he was only joking." Simone reached out, grabbing his arm, but he shrugged her hand away.

"Let me do my job."

She pressed her lips into a frown and watched him walk into her boss' office. Cranston followed him and she took up the rear.

Liam searched the office, opening the adjoining door that lead to a conference room and called it clear. "I'll leave you both to your meeting."

"Thank you," Simone said, glaring at him. As soon as her boss closed the door she said, "Sir, I'm sorry—"

"Don't apologize. He was only doing his job. I'm glad he takes protecting you seriously. I shouldn't have joked in the first place. Sit." Mr. Cranston motioned to the guest chair before he rounded his desk to sit down. "Let's discuss why I called you in this morning. I had a long talk with Hugh Webster of Webster-Reynolds yesterday. He told me you were less than attentive on your last meeting with them. I assured him this didn't sound like you at all and I'd get to the bottom of it. Is something wrong, Simone?"

There was concern in her boss's voice which was the last thing she'd expected when he called her in this morning. She'd come here prepared for a chewing out or at the least to be threatened with losing her job. His approach made her feel she had no choice but to be honest with him.

"My father is missing. His last known whereabouts was on business in DC. I didn't give Webster-Reynolds my fullest attention because all I could think about was that somewhere in the city my father could be dying alone if he'd been attacked or kidnapped. It's true, I have no proof of foul play, but I find it hard to swallow that people at his company are not concerned that he hasn't been heard from in all this time either."

"I see. I promised Webster-Reynolds you'd make this right. I planned to send you back there this week, but maybe that isn't the best idea. It sounds like you'll be just as distracted, especially now that you are also dealing with being a witness in this bar shooting."

"Actually, sir, getting out of town would be the best thing for me on that front. I wouldn't have to worry about that gang coming after me if I wasn't in town. And with Liam by my side, I'll stay focused on Webster-Reynolds during the day and we can search for my father in the evenings, if time allows."

"Are you sure, Simone?" Cranston asked. "If this goes south, your time here is over. You do understand?"

She slowly nodded. "I won't let you down, sir."

"Very well. Book flights for this afternoon and be ready for a week of making up."

"In other words, kissing up."

"I wouldn't say that, Simone."

"But it really is about stroking Webster-Reynolds's ego, isn't it?"

"Public relations. It's public relations."

"I won't let you down." She stood.

"See that you don't."

She heard the warning in his voice as she left the office, not fully relaxing until she was in the elevator, standing next to Liam. She avoided looking at him because she was afraid she'd say something she'd regret and she didn't really feel like arguing with him in public at the moment. They had too much to do to get ready for their flight.

"So?" Liam finally broke the silence.

"We're being sent to revisit Webster-Reynolds, the company I short changed with my attention when I was there last week. It will give us the opportunity to also look for my dad in the evenings. So it is a win-win if you ask me. I just have to stay focused during the day because my job is on the line. If Webster-Reynolds doesn't feel I am giving them 100% of my focus they will give a bad report to Mr. Cranston and I'm gone."

"I see. I'll let Hawkeye know we're leaving town and I'll text Brand, Will, and Wyatt as well. Do you know how long we'll be gone?"

"I flew back last Friday so we'll be gone all week. Five nights and four days."

"Roger that. Good thing I did my laundry last night."

Simone smiled at him as the elevator doors opened. He immediately called their driver and the SUV pulled around to get them.

SIMONE WAS able to book two business class shuttle tickets for later that afternoon. She called the same hotel she'd stayed at the week before and rebooked with them, requesting adjoining rooms. Then she threw together her suitcase and was ready to leave for the airport by the time Liam made the necessary phone calls to Chicago PD, Brand, Will and Wyatt.

On the ride to the airport she sent her mom a text that she was on another business trip and to call her cell if she needed to reach her. But in the pit of her stomach that just didn't seem enough. What if something bad happened to her while she was away from home? She had Liam with her, but still, he couldn't protect her every minute of the day.

"Everything okay?" He leaned toward her.

"Nerves before a flight."

"Yeah. Combat nerves. I get it."

She grinned.

At the airport they checked in. Liam checked his tactical bag and duffle. He showed the airport attendant papers that went with his bags. Simone wasn't sure what it was about; however, it didn't surprise her when the attendant tagged them with colored cable ties so they couldn't be opened during the flight. When it was her turn, Simone was still deep in thought and gave the woman her bag even though she hadn't planned to check it.

She followed Liam to security so they could be cleared to pass through to the waiting area. There was a short line, but they made it through with half an hour until their flight departed. They got coffee at the little kiosk and waited with the other commuters taking the shuttle flight from Chicago O'Hare to Washington National.

Simone sipped her coffee and sighed.

"It can't be that bad," he said.

"What?"

"Whatever has you so preoccupied?"

"I'm not..."

"Ah-ah-ah...You zoned out when we checked in upon our arrival. Don't deny it."

"So what? I've got a load on my mind with this revisit. I have to make a good impression on Webster-Reynolds or I'm out of a job."

"But that's not really what is on your mind."

"How can you be so sure of yourself?" She glanced at him and then at the sturdy disposable coffee container.

"Because the Simone I met Friday night doesn't let little trifles like impressions get to her. That's small potatoes to her. No. I'd say there is something more pressing on your mind."

She laughed at how well he could read her. Not even her friends knew her that well and they'd known her for years, but on that note she didn't want to admit he was right either. So she shrugged and went back to sipping her coffee.

"Simmering will only get your stomach in knots and make the flight unbearable. You might as well get it off your chest."

"I have nothing to get off my chest, thank you very much. Why don't you keep your nose out of my business for a change?"

"Testy. Tsk-tsk-tsk."

She rolled her eyes at him and swiveled in the seat so her back was to him. She tried to ignore him by looking at her phone, but she was all too aware of his body heat radiating off him from the seat beside her.

Thankfully their flight was called before her thoughts went south on body heat and close proximity. Of course, getting on a plane with Liam, thoughts of joining the mile high club kept running through her head as they boarded the plane and she had to tamp them down. There was no way she was luring him into the airplanes lavatory to join that club, as tempting as that thought was at the moment.

She didn't understand what had suddenly gotten into her. Had there been something spicy in her coffee?

"Let me have your laptop bag and I'll stow it in the overhead compartment," Liam said.

Slipping it off her shoulder, she was careful not to let their fingers touch in the exchange. Contact with him right now might send a ripple effect down her body. She quickly took her seat beside the window and got comfortable, putting her purse under the seat in front of her.

Liam put the arm rest up between their seats before he sat down. "Hope you don't mind. Those are annoying as all get out."

"No. Not at all."

"Good. Do you have your notes on your last trip so I can go over where you looked for your dad? I'd like to think about a strategy during the flight."

"S-sure." She got the notepad out of her purse and handed it to him, then stared out the window waiting for the plane to start moving for take-off. When that time came, she leaned her head back and laid her right hand on the arm rest, but her left made contact with Liam's arm instead. She immediately looked at him and smiled as the plane rose into the air and made its ascent to flying altitude. Then she removed it as nonchalantly as she could, settling in for their flight.

LIAM STUDIED the notes Simone had taken on what she'd learned of her father's last whereabouts while in Washington, DC. She'd been thorough in her search for him. He found they even drew the same conclusions, as her side notes indicated in the margins. Yet her father, Clayton Reid, was nowhere to be found. But he planned to change that outcome on this trip, or at least have a better sense of what might have happened to the man. There had to be a lead that was not uncovered in the nations' capitol.

As soon as their flight touched down and the pilot

thanked them for flying with the airlines, they got off the plane and made their way to baggage claim. Simone's bag was waiting for her there, but he had to go to the security office to get his released to him because of the nature of its contents. He left her momentarily, and when he returned, she looked upset.

"What's wrong?"

"Our hotel. There was a malfunction with the sprinkler system on two of the floors. They are having to reroute guests to different hotels for their stay. They say at no additional cost, but this hotel was business class and a perfect location for Webster-Reynolds. Plus, I booked us adjoining rooms. We might not get that where they are sending us."

"You don't know that for sure. As we learned in the marines, go with the flow. Don't assume the worst until your staring the worst in the face. Then think about the brighter side."

She tried to smile at him. "Thanks, but it still doesn't help. I'm a creature of habit. I always stay at that hotel when I come on business for Webster-Reynolds. I know my way around when I'm there. This move will throw everything off for me."

She grabbed the handle of her rolling bag and shook all over. "Get a grip, Simone. You're a big girl. You can do this. Stop complaining."

Now that wasn't something he'd expected from her.

"Let's get a cab," he said.

"No. Metro. It'll be faster."

"Cab. Safer."

She chuckled. "Right. And get stuck in DC traffic. Metro this way."

She started walking toward the exit and he followed. If she wanted to walk however many blocks to the metro station in high heels she could be his guest; he was thinking about her comfort. He, on the other hand, could handle walking anywhere in the city.

As it turned out the metro station was outside the airport, so they didn't have to go far and they took the blue line over to McPherson Square where they got off and walked less than a block to the hotel.

SIMONE LOOKED up at the façade of the hotel and sucked in her breath. This was definitely classier than the hotel she had booked, but if they were covering the charges for her stay, she wasn't about to complain. Before she could open the door, a bellman came out and held the door for her and Liam to enter.

"Thank you," she said.

"My pleasure. Enjoy your stay."

They crossed the atrium to the front desk and she was very aware of the click, click of her heels on the polished, marble floor and the whir, whir of the wheels on her roll-along.

"Welcome, are you checking in?" the front desk clerk asked.

"Yes. I should have a reservation under Reid. Simone Reid. Two connecting king rooms transferred from the Belmonté."

"Reid. Yes, I do see a reservation for you, but I'm afraid

we do not have any connecting rooms available. We have a junior suite for you instead. It's on the concierge level and you'll have access to all the concierge amenities for the duration of your stay."

"How many rooms does the suite have?" Simone asked.

"One king bed, private sitting area with French doors," the clerk explained.

"That won't work. We need two rooms," Simone said.

"I can sleep anywhere." Liam leaned closer to her. "It'll be fine. What kind of sofa is in the room, ma'am?"

The clerk looked at him. "It isn't a sofa sleeper, sir. The sitting area is for meetings or entertaining."

"I don't understand why the Belmonté wouldn't transfer my reservation here for the same as I had? Two rooms, whether connecting or not."

"One reservation. One room," the clerk explained.

Simone shook her head. "That still isn't solving the problem. We need two beds. Couldn't you change my reservation to a room with two queens or something?"

"I'm sorry. We're booked. The junior suite is an upgrade at no extra charge."

"It's fine. I can sleep on the floor if I have to."

Simone turned to him. "No you won't. I booked you a room and you are not going to sleep on the floor."

She turned back to the clerk and smiled, sweetly, keeping her voice calm. "What about a rollaway? Can you send one of those to the room for him?"

"No ma'am we do not have rollaway beds here."

"That stinks." Her voice rose an octave.

"Simone. It's fine. I can sleep anywhere."

"Do you want the junior suite or not?" The clerk sounded irritated at the discussion.

"Yes. We'll take it under the circumstances, but I'm not happy."

The clerk handed them their room keys and they walked to the bank of elevators. Stepping inside, Simone looked at Liam. "The king bed is large enough for both of us. We'll just make a wall down the middle with pillows or an extra blanket. You stay on your side. I'll stay on my side. End of discussion."

"If that's how you want it."

"I just said so, didn't I?"

"You did." He shook his head, smiling.

It irked her that he found their situation amusing. But it kinda was, after all. She was the one having thoughts of joining the mile high club with him on the airplane. And because of this snafu with the hotel room she could easily find herself waking up across the blanket border curled up next to him. Or even worse, what if she had a wild dream about him or something and acted on it in the middle of the night? This could be dangerous territory she was walking into, but his friends called him Don Juan for a reason. It had to be other than his last name being Donovan. Perhaps it was time to put him to the test.

CHAPTER 8

Night one in the junior suite

Liam slept better than he expected even though, when he woke up at one point during the night he was more than aware of Simone being across that blanket barrier she'd insisted on. She snored. Not loud. Softly, like a mewling kitten. It was cute.

He'd lain there for a while listening to her until her leg shifted, crossing the blanket and brushed his thigh. His groin instantly hardened, a reaction he hadn't expected from such a simple touch. This couldn't be happening. Not here. Not now with Simone. Brand had already warned him to keep his libido in check. And he intended to do just that, even if he was forced to share this bed with her every night while at this hotel. He would *not* cross the line. This was a job. Not a hookup. No matter how many times her leg brushed his during the night or her tight bottom bumped up against him in sleep, he would remain neutral, even if it killed him.

He'd rolled over, punched his pillow and tried his best

to go back to sleep, but it wasn't easy. Just knowing Simone was inches away and he couldn't touch her made the junior suite feel like the worst torture chamber he'd ever been trapped in. And he'd thought his room at Walter Reed had been tight quarters and a death sentence. If he had only known then what he was going through now? He'd relish his recovery time after Helmand.

When he finally woke the next morning, it was too early. Simone was rushing around the room, trying to get ready because she'd overslept from what he heard her mumbling. He laid there, watching her try to be quiet, but she was doing a lousy job at it. She even tripped over his tactical bag and he had it tucked out of the way, or so he thought. When she was finally ready to leave, she grabbed her purse and computer bag and left, letting the suite door close loudly behind her. He heard her curse out in the hallway and he chuckled.

He rolled over and went back to sleep for a couple more hours before he finally got up and started his day. Then he got ready and went down to the concierge desk to inquire about the best local hangouts and a map of the city.

"The local hangouts? As opposed to where tourists go?" the man at the desk asked.

"That's right. I've found that the locals know better and visit the smaller, off the beaten path places in cities."

"This is DC. You can't go wrong either local or tourist."

"That may be true, but I still like to check out the local favorites whenever I travel."

"Okay. I'd go down to K Street and check out Oliver's.

If you time it right you'll get a table. If not, you might get an order to go, but the line may be too long. It really depends on the time you go."

"I hear you. That sounds like the place I'm looking for. Thanks. And thanks for the metro and city maps." Liam gave him a five dollar tip for his help before heading out of the hotel. He went straight to K Street to beat the local crowd for lunch and got a table at Oliver's.

Simone had shared a photo of her father on his phone, so he showed the image of Clayton Reid to the waitress before the lunch crowd got heavy. He was curious if the man might have frequented the place on his trips to DC, but she was new to the area and had only worked there a few weeks. She sent over the manager and Liam showed Clayton's photo to her, but she didn't recognize him either as a regular customer.

Liam ordered the lunch special and enjoyed every bite of the lasagna, garlic bread and salad. He even finished it off with tiramisu. Totally sated, he paid for his meal and headed to his next destination, the hotel where Clayton Reid had checked in, but never checked out. Simone had requested they keep his luggage until he showed back up and had even paid them a deposit to store it for sixty days. So Liam just needed to ask the manager a few questions that perhaps Simone didn't cover when she spoke with them. And see if he could take a look at hotel security video with his Chicago PD clearance. It was a long shot, but he'd put a call in to Hawkeye if he needed to see if he could pull a few strings.

A man Clayton Reid's age and business status didn't just vanish without a trace in this day and age of electronic footprint. Unless he wasn't missing at all. That was an angle Liam hadn't thought through. What if the man had taken himself off the grid for a reason? It was a theory worth investigating if the other didn't pan out, but for now he'd follow up with the hotel manager and make a phone call to Reid's secretary to see what he could learn from her as well.

The Hotel Palomar was a modern hotel that catered more to Liam and Simone's age group than he suspected to Clayton Reid, yet according to Simone's notes, this was the hotel her father stayed at every time he came to DC. It was located on P Street near DuPont Circle. He wasn't sure what the appeal was to the hotel. Location? Night life? Museums? Art Galleries?

"What secrets are you keeping Clayton Reid?" Liam asked, standing in the atrium of the Palomar taking it all in. He noticed a display for loaner bikes. An Italian restaurant on site called to him even though he had only just eaten. The aroma of pasta and spices had him walking over to the glass encased menu outside the restaurant. He looked it over and made a quick decision.

"Do you take reservations?" He asked the hostess on duty.

"We do. What size of a party will you be having?"

"Two for dinner this evening. Do you have an opening for 7:30?"

"Yes. I can put you down for then. What name?" she asked.

"Donovan. Liam Donovan."

"I have you down, Mr. Donovan."

"Excellent." He walked over to the front desk and asked to speak to the hotel manager.

"Is there anything I can help you with?" the clerk asked. He was a gentleman who looked to be in his mid-thirties.

"No. It's a matter about a guest who never checked out." Liam flashed him his Chicago PD credentials. "I think the manager is the best person to speak with about the situation."

"Certainly." The man picked up a phone and made a call. When he hung up, he looked back at Liam. "She'll be right with you."

"Thank you." Liam stepped away from the counter so anyone wanting to check-in could do it while he waited.

"I'm Shelby Mitchell, day manager. How can I help you?"

"I'm Liam Donovan with Chicago PDs Protection Task Force." He flashed his credentials for her, then he pulled up the picture of Simone's father on his phone. "I'm here to ask you a few questions about this man, Clayton Reid. I understand he was staying here when he went missing?"

The woman paled and motioned him to follow her over to a seating area. "I'd rather not have other guests over hear this conversation. I do not believe that Mr. Reid's disappearance has anything to do with the Palomar. He stays here when he is in DC. He's a lovely man. Older than most of our guests, but he never appeared out of place here. He fit in, if you know what I mean. I spoke to his daughter only last week and told her I knew nothing about his going missing. When he did not check out as scheduled and his room wasn't emptied, housekeeping did pack his bags. We held them as a courtesy for him, thinking he got held up in a business meeting and didn't get to return on time. That has happened before. But he has always returned to collect his baggage."

"Did you tell his daughter that?" Liam asked.

"I'm not sure. She was distraught over her father being missing when she came and found he had not come back to collect his luggage or check. She paid a deposit and arrangements for us to keep the bags here until he returned."

Liam nodded. "During the time Mr. Reid stayed here can you recall him ever having a meeting here with anyone that looked suspicious?"

"No. To my recollection he never met anyone here. He never brought anyone back to the hotel with him either."

"Did you by chance report him missing to the Washington police?" Liam asked.

"No."

"Don't you think you should have?"

The woman chewed on her bottom lip for a moment. "Yes. I guess we should have. Or I should have, but after speaking with his daughter, I felt it was up to her to pursue matters further. Not the hotel."

"Of course you would. After all, calling the police in and having to admit you allowed housekeeping to clean a possible crime scene of any evidence left behind would have surely looked like you had been trying to cover up something."

"That's unfair, Mr. Donovan. At that point we had no idea that Mr. Reid was even missing. How could we have known the room could be a potential crime scene? He was due to check out."

"I'm sorry. You are correct. That was highly off the cuff and unfair for me to say. We should all have hindsight. Still the man has been missing now for close to a month and no one is the wiser because it wasn't reported to Washington PD. If his daughter hadn't taken it upon herself to come looking and reported to us, this little investigation wouldn't be happening now. This could be a cold case due to negligence."

"Negligence? You don't think Ms. Reid will try to sue us?"

A lawsuit wasn't the button he was trying to push. He'd only wanted the woman to realize she should have called authorities immediately.

"I can't speak for Ms. Reid, but I believe what she really wants is her father safely found."

"Let's hope. Is there anything else you'd like to know?" Ms. Mitchell asked.

"Did you look at security tapes around the time Mr. Reid stayed here to make sure he wasn't abducted outside the hotel? Or from his room?"

"No, we didn't."

"I don't suppose I can take a look at the tapes from the time he stayed?" Liam asked.

"You could, but they are recycled after thirty days."

"Of course."

But it hasn't really been thirty days.

"Thank you for your time. I do appreciate it. If I need to follow up on anything I may drop back by," he said.

"Sure. We really wish Mr. Reid well, wherever he may be."

He left the hotel and walked to the corner, taking the alley down to the back of the hotel and checking for ways anyone could get into the establishment without being seen. He spotted the surveillance cameras, so the place was covered, if Reid was abducted it would have been on the video footage. If the hotel didn't rerecord over it every thirty days. Sixty would be a better policy, but he wasn't in charge.

Satisfied with what he found, he headed back to the street and to the closest metro station. He stopped at a newspaper stand and picked up the day's edition, since he had a good ten-minute ride to his next destination.

He purchased his fare at the kiosk and went through the turnstile before going into the tunnel to wait for the train. Then he got on the red line that would take him to Metro City and his destination. He settled in for the ride, looking through the paper until he found an article on Lincler Technologies and Securities that interested him. The company name sounded familiar and he wasn't sure why, until he saw a former marine buddy, Sam Jensen's name in the article. According to the reporter, Jensen was a junior executive there, proving he'd done well for himself after Helmand. He'd not been injured during deployment and when the tour was over, he'd been discharged and moved on with his life.

Liam pulled out his notepad and jotted down Sam's name as a reminder to follow up with him if he got a chance before leaving town. He continued reading the article and discovered that the securities division did much the same as the Brotherhood Protectors, except without employing wounded veterans.

He wouldn't waste his time dwelling on what could have been. He'd made a fresh start after recovering with Hank Patterson and the Brotherhood team. He didn't regret for a minute accepting the strange offer he'd received while at Walter Reed from Leigha Nipton, his physical therapist who'd acted as a recruiter, for lack of better name for it. She'd worked with him until he was ready to manage on his own, then she'd approached him about working for Hank. The next thing he knew, Hank was there in person talking up the Brotherhood Protectors and how Liam could come to The Better Days Ranch to finish recouping and get his strength back before starting to really work for him.

Looking back, it all still seemed too good to be true yet it had been three years since he joined up. Another eight months before he met Brand and Will. Wyatt had been the last of their crew to come along, having spent time training as a counselor for those suffering from PTSD after suffering from it himself.

A light blinked above the door on the metro car, flashing the name of the station they were coming into and Liam folded up the newspaper ready to get off. He made his way to the escalator leading to the street level and crossed at the first available light.

He walked a block and then entered one of the taller buildings on the block. According to Simone's notes this was the location of her father's last meeting before he went missing. Clayton Reid had met with Testermen

International about shipping and receiving of goods for one of his clients, Samwell Brady.

He walked to the large directory of businesses located in the building, but didn't find Testerman International listed. There was a blank space as if a name had recently been removed from the felt board behind the glass pane. He turned and looked at the security desk, then double checked his notes that he was at the right address before he bothered the guard on duty.

"Excuse me, sir, but could you tell me if I'm in the right building. I'm looking for Testerman International."

The guard grinned. "You and half a dozen others that come through here. They were a short-term lease and they cleared out of here faster than any legitimate business I've ever seen."

"So you are saying they weren't on the up and up?" Liam asked.

The man shrugged. "Appearance is what it is."

"Maybe you can tell me if you ever saw this man come through here before Testerman left the building. I know it might be a long shot. You have to see hundreds of people walk in here daily." Liam pulled up Clayton Reid's photo on his phone and showed it the man.

"There was a girl in here last week asking about him. A real pretty young woman too. Said she was his daughter. I told her I remembered seeing him and I've thought about it since then and I'm certain I saw him come here three times. Once right after Testerman moved in. Another two months later."

"And the last?" Liam held his breath afraid of when the man would say.

"I think it was about a month ago. Right before Testerman slowly slipped out of the premises. But if you are really interested in knowing more about Testerman, you should talk to the building manager." The guard opened up a desk drawer and pulled out a card. "Tawanda Ford at Lincler Properties."

"Lincler?" Liam said.

"That's right. Lincler is the new kid on the block, and the hottest commodity right now in DC. Lincler has its hands into everything."

Hmm. Lincler Technologies and Securities? Lincler Properties? Not a coincidence from what the guard was saying, so there was definitely a connection. Maybe he needed to make sure he paid his old pal Sam Jensen a visit for sure while he was in DC.

"Thanks for the card and the tip. I'll be sure to check in with Ms. Ford. You have a good afternoon." Liam put the card in his pocket then headed to the street and the nearest coffee shop. He needed caffeine and to mull this information over. He also needed a quiet place where he could give Clayton Reid's administrative assistant a call.

Finding a coffee shop wasn't difficult, since there were several to choose from, one every other block. But, he decided to hop on the metro and head back toward the hotel so he'd be close when he finished for the day.

He took the blue line toward McPherson Square and went to one called Zeke's, because it reminded him of another marine buddy that didn't make it out of Helmand. Zeke's proclaimed to roast their coffee beans in DC. It was a small shop with stools and high top tables. Liam got his coffee and found a spot away from the few people in the shop so he had privacy to make the call.

Edna Kravitz answered on the second ring. "Clayton Reid's office, Edna speaking."

"Hello, Edna, my name is Liam Donovan, I'm with the Chicago PD's Protection Task Force. I am trying to track down Mr. Reid. I understand he has not been in the office in several weeks. Can you answer a few questions for me?"

"Why is the Chicago PD interested in the whereabouts of Mr. Reid? Oh, it's his daughters doing, isn't it? I told her when I talked to her that it wasn't unusual for him to go off the radar for weeks at a time, but I could tell she wasn't happy about it. I'm sure he will turn up eventually. He always does with a new account to his credit."

"So you believe this is all in the nature of business? That he isn't really missing, but pursuing a new client lead and forgot to check out of his hotel in DC? He just left his belongings at the Palomar?"

"Well...I can't speak to that, but he has always turned up in the past. One would assume that would still be the case now."

"Edna. You do know what they say about people who assume?" Liam said, pausing for effect.

"Mr. Donovan, I do. All I can tell you is his business practices are unique and unlike any other man I've worked for in my thirty odd years as an administrative assistant, but he is fair and compensates me well for my time. I can't complain."

"Can I leave you my number in the event he should show up at the office? I am in DC trying to track him

DON JUAN

down. I'd like to speak with him at the earliest if he should happen to walk through the door."

"Certainly."

"555-276-4663."

"I've got it, Mr. Donovan."

"Thank you, Edna. I know Simone appreciates it."

He hung up and drank his coffee, rereading the article on Lincler Technologies and Securities, keeping in mind what the security guard had told him about Lincler having its hands into everything. He did a quick search on his phone and came up with a number for the company. He jotted that down beside Sam Jensen's name in his notebook before he headed back to the hotel.

CHAPTER 9

SIMONE RUSHED through the door of the junior suite, about to hyperventilate. She couldn't get her breath no matter what she did. It was a wonder she had been able to make it back to the Hamilton without passing out after receiving the video of her father gagged and bound by the kidnappers. Thankfully, her meeting with Webster-Reynolds had already ended for the day, so they weren't any wiser to her personal life crashing in around her.

She kicked off her heels and fell onto the sofa, flopping backwards, staring up at the ceiling. It took several moments for her heart to stop pounding and for her to be able to breathe normally. Tears ran down her face, but her voice was inaudible. She couldn't move. It was like she was frozen and her chest hurt something fierce, like an elephant was sitting on it.

The door to the suite opened and she prayed it was Liam coming in and that she hadn't left it ajar for a stranger to walk in on her in this vulnerable state. She couldn't protect herself if someone were to attack her at that moment. It was humiliating that Liam had to see her like this right now, but he had already found her having a meltdown in the shower.

"Simone? Are you okay?" Liam called from across the room. "Simone, are you asleep?"

She tried to move her head to look at him, but it was useless. A single tear rolled from her eye, back into her hairline and down her neck. It hung there for the longest time before it dropped. As if setting off a ripple effect, her cellphone slipped from her fingers and onto the carpeted floor. She hadn't even realized she was still holding it.

A shadow moved close to her, but she couldn't look away from the ceiling where her eyes were focused.

"Simone. Can you hear me?" Liam held her phone in her line of sight. "I'm looking at your phone, so don't get mad at me. I've warned you before doing it."

He kicked the small coffee table and she heard him curse under his breath before he came back into sight. He was standing over her, closer this time so all she could see was his face. "Breathe. Just breathe. You're going to be okay. It's a panic attack. I've had them before, after my accident in Helmand. You'll get through this. If you don't breathe I'm going to have to call for an ambulance and that means I'll have to cancel our dinner reservations tonight. And I really wanted Italian food."

He was grinning when he said that so she knew he was joking, trying to get her to smile, but she also saw the concern in his warm brown eyes and heard it in his voice.

"Honey, come on now, you have to breathe through it. It won't pass it if you don't."

She tried, she really did. She'd been trying ever since this 'panic' attack started.

He made a phone call and she thought he really was calling for an ambulance, but then she heard him say "Wyatt." He walked far enough away from her that she couldn't make out what he was saying. Besides, she was having a hard enough time focusing on breathing at the moment, because the elephant on her chest had gained another hundred pounds.

Images of her father flashed before he eyes, gagged and blindfolded, and the kidnapper's voice telling her she had twenty-four hours to get one million in unmarked bills to them, and not to go to the authorities or her father was dead. She knew that Liam had that information now, because he'd watched the video and he was talking to Wyatt. That meant Will and Brand would know soon enough. How was she supposed to keep the authorities from getting involved when Liam was working for the Chicago PD? Sure he was in Washington DC, but she doubted Chicago had much jurisdiction in another state, let alone the nation's capital.

The thought of her father being killed because they didn't follow the kidnappers' instructions freed her from the invisible bond that had her immobile. She sat up and screamed. "NO!"

LIAM DROPPED HIS PHONE. He pivoted around, forgetting about Wyatt on the line and rushed over to the sofa where Simone sat, screaming at the top of her lungs. He didn't know if she was hurt and from what he recalled from his own therapy for panic attacks, nothing like this was ever covered. Wyatt had had very little time to advise him on anything.

He pulled her to him and tried to comfort her, rocking her back and forth. "Sh-h-h. It's gonna be okay. We'll find your father. We'll get the money somehow and we'll meet the kidnappers' demands. Don't worry. I've been on hostage recovery missions before. I know what to do."

She stopped screaming, but shook her head. "No authorities. They said come alone."

He placed his hands on her cheeks, holding her head still, so he could examine her eyes to make sure she wasn't in shock and that she was comprehending what he was saying. Her pupils looked normal, no dilation. "You can do it alone, but I am with you on this one. Don't forget that."

"How? How are we going to pull it off without the kidnappers finding out and killing him? How?" She blinked several times and sniffled, which was a good sign for someone who had been frozen stiff a few moments ago.

"Let me worry about the how. You worry about nothing right now except continuing to breathe in and out. Turn around, put your feet up on the couch and relax while I go finish my call to Wyatt."

"He can't get involved—"

"I didn't call him about your father, Simone. I called him about you, to ask what I needed to do to help you through the panic attack."

"Oh."

Hearing that put her at ease. She wilted against the

sofa, not saying another word. He waited a couple of heart beats before he left her in the event she should reconsider, but she didn't. Thankfully, the line was still active.

"Are you still there?" Liam asked, putting the phone to his ear.

"Was that Simone screaming? Is she okay?"

"Yes and yes. I called about a panic attack she was having, but she broke through it right as you answered the phone. Sorry about that. We received rather disturbing news this afternoon about her father."

"I see. Anything I can do to help?"

"No. I'm sure you have more than enough to deal with on your end. Are you still residing at the hospital with Colleen?"

"Actually we are heading home this evening. Or rather we have an evening flight to Montana. I'm taking her to Better Days to recuperate. I think a few days with my Ruby will do her some good."

"Not to mention that Montana mountain fresh air."

"Don't make me homesick," Wyatt said.

Liam grinned, turning around to check on Simone. She had her eyes closed and her breathing looked normal. He had a funny feeling she may have dosed off to sleep. He was going to have to cancel their dinner reservations, but that was okay. Perhaps they could go another night before they left town.

"Sorry buddy. I know how much you like it there."

"I thought you were liking it too?"

"I was. I do. It's different from Oklahoma, but I've found I can make home wherever I lay my head, too. You call if you need anything. I'll be on the next plane out, even if I have to drag Simone with me."

Wyatt snorted. "I can just picture that now."

"My dragging her with me?"

"Yes and her at Better Days trying to fit in."

Liam thought about it, too. The picture of her in faded blue jeans and a t-shirt with her hair braided in pigtails, sticking out from under a straw cowboy hat while she sat on a horse was appealing.

"You never know. It could happen."

"I'll believe it when I see it," Wyatt said. "I better go. The nurse just came in with the discharge paperwork. It looks like we're finally outta here."

"Travel safe." Liam ended the call and did a quick search for the Palomar so he could cancel his dinner reservations. When he finished he turned around and found Simone staring at him.

"Why'd you do that?"

"I didn't think you'd feel up to going out tonight after your panic attack. We can do it later in the week if we have time. If not, it isn't the end of the world," he said.

"But you sounded like you really wanted to go there when you first told me about it."

"I did, but your health is more important than my stomach getting Italian food. We can order in a pizza and I'll be just as happy."

She smiled. "Pizza sounds divine and thanks for understanding. I don't think my legs would allow me to stand right now. They feel immobile."

"It's the aftermath of the panic attack. It'll wear off."

"Can you hand me my phone. I need to call my mom. I

need to see if she received the same ransom demand as I did."

"Why do you think the kidnappers would contact her if your parents are divorced and she's remarried?" Liam asked.

"Because my step-father, Leland Stanwell, is a very wealthy real-estate developer. He's accrued more money than my father over the years. And even though he has semi-retired since they moved to Miami, he is still very active in the real-estate game."

"I guess the big question here is whether or not you have access to your father's money in order to pay the ransom demand?" Liam asked.

"I do and I don't. If something should happen to my father it becomes mine as stipulated in his will. However, before then I have to go through his attorney, to give me immediate power of attorney which means I'd have to get another person involved."

Liam handed her phone to her. "Then call your mom. Though I think if the kidnappers had reached out to her, she'd have already contacted you, don't you think?"

"Maybe. Maybe not."

He watched as Simone dialed the number, then he heard a woman sobbing on the other end of the line when the call connected.

"Mom, what's wrong? What's happened?" Simone demanded, putting the call on speaker.

"I thought you'd been shot! I got a video of your father last night demanding money immediately and when we didn't pay, I got another video of you with a guy pointing a gun at you and pulling the trigger and you dropping to the floor. I thought we'd killed you because we refused to meet their demands. They wanted five million dollars in two hours, but we couldn't get that amount to them that fast. I mean, who keeps that amount of money accessible?"

"That video must have been of me at the bar last Friday night. Those SOBs."

"Mrs. Stanwell, I'm Liam Donovan. I've been assigned to protect your daughter by the Chicago PD. Can you forward your video to her phone so we can compare what was sent to you to the video she received from the kidnappers? They wanted her to pay one million for her father in twenty-four hours."

"Protection? Simone, you didn't tell me you had been given protection after that bar shooting."

"I'm okay mom. Everything is fine. Other than dad missing now."

"How do I know this Liam Donovan is really not one of the kidnappers who is holding you hostage?"

"Fair enough, Mrs. Stanwell. You can call her friend Jules and check with her. My buddy Will has been assigned to protect her. They can vouch for me. We're all part of the same protection task force," Liam explained.

"Mom, really? Don't go getting all paranoid on me, just because I didn't tell you everything after the bar shooting. I didn't want to worry you by telling you about the protection detail to keep me safe."

"And don't you think I had a right to know that, Simone? I thought we had a better relationship than you keeping that a secret from me."

"Sorry, Mom..."

"Sorry isn't going to cut it. It was little things like that …"

"I know. I know. That's how things went sour with you and dad." Simone turned away from Liam, twisting strands of her hair around her finger. "You've told me several times how I have to be careful because I'm not just part you, I'm also part of him too. But, mom, I am a grown woman and I am capable of taking care of myself and deciding what to tell you, and what not to tell you about my life."

"Not when it comes down to you being held at gunpoint, Simone. I don't care if you're sixty-two and I'm over 100 years old and senile. I want to know even if I can't comprehend what you're telling me. I'm your mother."

Simone broke into a smile. "I understand that mom."

"Now, Mr. Donovan, you take care of my daughter. Don't let anything happen to her or I'll hunt you down."

"I believe you would, Mrs. Stanwell."

"I'm sending the video when I hang up. Don't pay the ransom. Your father has done something to get into this mess. Let him get himself out of it."

"Mom, I can't do that. What if they kill him?"

There was a long pause.

"You do what you have to do, Simone, just be careful doing it."

The line went dead.

"Jiminy."

CHAPTER 10

NIGHT two in the junior suite

Simone tossed and turned, unable to sleep. It wasn't because of Liam being in bed with her on the other side of the blanket barrier. It was because she'd not been able to reach her dad's attorney to get access to the ransom money. He had already left the office by the time she called, and his secretary would not forward her call. It had not mattered that Simone explained it was a life and death situation. Apparently, all his clients claimed that on a regular basis. Instead, the woman had taken Simone's information and assured her he'd return her call tomorrow. Maybe her mom had been right—paying the ransom was a big mistake.

But what kind of trouble could her father have gotten himself into? And why would the gang members who shot up the Pied Piper bar be involved in it?

She was surprised that Liam hadn't realized that after her mother sent the video of her fake shooting. He transferred it to his laptop and they'd watched it several times, comparing it with the one Simone had received.

Maybe he had realized the gang was involved in the kidnapping, but didn't say anything so not to panic me?

Turning over toward him, she couldn't believe he was lying there sleeping when she was having such difficulty. She kicked the sheet off of her. But all that did was allow the few rays of moonlight that drifted through the window to illuminate Liam's bare chest, making his tanned skin radiate against the white sheets.

A groan escaped her and she quickly covered her mouth with her right hand afraid he might have heard her and wake up.

"What did I tell you about looking at me like I'm man candy, Simone?" He didn't even open his eyes to look at her.

"How do you know I'm staring at you?"

"I can feel it. Roll over and go to sleep. There is nothing we can do about your father tonight."

"I can't, Liam. I can't stop thinking about him and what the kidnappers might be doing to him."

He turned onto his side, finally opening his eyes. "Did your father look hurt in the video?"

"No."

"Exactly. They had him blindfolded, gagged and his hands tied behind his back. That is all. He was sitting in a chair. The room he was in was dark so we couldn't tell where he was located, but it looked decent. He was well groomed, so they were taking good care of him. After all, he's been missing for several weeks. For all we know they bound him for the video and let him lose afterwards."

"But—"

"No, we aren't going to go there, thinking the worst and worrying over what we can't control. We are going to take care of ourselves, sleep and eat and be well-rested so we can do our best come tomorrow. So come here." He reached his arm out and motioned for her to come toward him.

"What?"

"Just come here."

She wasn't sure what he had in mind, but she slowly moved toward him. She watched as he removed the blanket barrier they'd used the night before out of the bed. He patted the spot for her where the blanket had been.

"Don't be afraid. Just lay here and we'll go back to sleep together."

She swallowed, not sure that was going to help her any, but she did what he asked, turning on her side so her back was to him. He pulled the sheet up to her waist before he curled up behind her and let his arm fall over her hip.

"Good night, Simone."

"Good night, Liam."

She closed her eyes, amazed that feeling his warm breath on the back of her neck wasn't driving her crazy. Instead it made her feel protected and she soon fell asleep.

THE ALARM SOUNDED WAY TOO EARLY the next morning. She turned it off and went back to sleep, but then her phone was ringing. She reached for it afraid it was her dad's lawyer calling.

"Hello?"

"Simone, it's your mom. Hope I didn't wake you. I know it's early, but I wanted to catch you before you left for work."

"Uh-huh."

"I hated the way we left things yesterday. I had the hardest time sleeping last night."

"Me too."

"You should pay the ransom. After all, it's your father's money. If he has done something that he owes these kidnappers for, then you should pay them."

"Really? I'm glad you said that because I can't just *not* pay it. I have to get my father back."

"I know you do, honey. I also think you need to ignore what the kidnappers want and go to the authorities. This is not something you should be doing on your own."

Simone threw the sheet back and sat up. "I'm not on my own mom, I have a former Marine with me. He might not be the former Navy Seal like Carly got, but Liam's still top notch or he wouldn't have been chosen to be a Brotherhood Protector. He'll not let anything happen to me. You can count on that."

Simone felt the mattress shift behind her. Liam was awake. *Had he heard what she'd said about him?* Of course he had. How could he not have?

"I don't know what you're talking about," her mother said. "Brotherhood what? Last night your said protection task force? Which is it?"

"Both. The guys were Brotherhood Protectors out of

Montana until they came to Chicago and started working with the local PD, and now they are a special protection task force. They report to Commander Burns with the Chicago PD. He was a former Seal with Brand Chambers."

"And you say Brand is assigned to your friend Carly?"

"Yes. Carly and I were in the bar when the shooting took place. We were eye witnesses." Simone got off the bed and went toward the bathroom to start getting ready for her day.

"And where was Colleen during all of this? I know Jules was there because you already said she has a protector, too."

"Yes, Jules was outside going to catch the "L" when she heard the gunshots and came running back toward the bar, but she never made it inside. Which, now that I think about it doesn't make sense. She couldn't have been that far away. And if she came running back to the bar, what took her so long to get there? Liam and Brand said that a detective was preventing her from entering the bar when they arrived."

"I don't know, honey, maybe that is something you need to ask Jules about yourself."

"Yeah. I think I will if I ever get to see her. I haven't. In fact she is the only one I haven't seen. Carly and I got away from Brand and Liam on Saturday and went to the hospital to see Colleen. They were not happy about that."

"Simone, why was Colleen in the hospital? What haven't you told me about that night?"

She inhaled. "Colleen was attacked when she went to the ladies room. We didn't know it. Carly and I were dealing with the shooting in the bar and Colleen was being beaten by some creep in the ladies. Her face took the worst of it, but thankfully when he heard the gunshot, it scared him away and he didn't do more to her."

"Oh my God. That poor sweet girl. I'll have to call Joan. She does know doesn't she?"

"Yes, mom. Bob and Joan were called to the hospital right away. They were there for Colleen and she's been assigned someone to protect her, too."

"I think I'm getting on the next flight to Chicago. Leland and I both will."

"Have fun because I'm not there, remember. I'm in DC for the week. And if you come, you'll have to stay at a hotel because Liam has the guest room."

"Oh, that's right. Well maybe we should come to DC instead. I just really want to be with you wherever you are right now. I want to hold my daughter and know she is safe."

"I am, and you can as soon as we find dad and get back to Chicago."

"We're still coming to DC. We'll be at the Willard if we can get a room. That is where Leland and I always stay."

"Okay. I'll talk to you later then." Simone ended the call.

Liam came around the corner with one eyebrow raised. "I take it she's coming here?"

"The city, not the hotel. I couldn't talk her out of it."

"Not a good idea. We don't know if the kidnappers are still in DC or if they have your father elsewhere. If your mother and Leland come here, that could make them sitting ducks as well."

Panic for her mom and Leland's safety set in and the

next thing Simone knew the room began to spin as her vision narrowed, before she lost sight altogether. Then she was coming around, laying on the bed while Liam waved something putrid underneath her nose.

"What's that smell?" She pushed his hand away.

"Smelling salts."

She tried to sit up, but weakly fell back against the pillows. She covered her hand over her mouth because she felt sick for a moment, but that soon passed.

"You're white as a sheet, Simone. You're not going anywhere this morning. You need to lie still and rest. I'll call Webster-Reynolds and tell them you won't be in until this afternoon."

"I can't. I have meetings with them."

"You can and you will. If they can't understand you getting ill, then I'll call your boss and let him make the call to them."

"Perhaps that is best. I don't understand what is wrong with me. I never pass out. Now I've done that and had a panic attack in less than eighteen hours. I have a splitting headache and I feel nauseated."

"Exactly. That is what is wrong with you. Your body has been through trauma whether you realize it or not. Your nervous system cannot handle this much stress and bounce back so easily. Think about everything that has happened to you since Friday night, and its only Tuesday."

She closed her eyes and groaned. "Don't remind me."

"I'm going to use your phone to call Cranston. Don't get up."

Simone lay there waiting for the stomach to stop rolling, then she noticed she was extremely thirsty. She called to Liam, but he didn't hear her since he was in the outer room. She tried to raise up, but that made her feel ill again, so she scooted to the edge of the bed and slipped off into the floor.

Technically she wasn't up, she was down, and she really wanted a cold bottle of water out of the little refrigerator that was just outside the French doors separating the bedroom from the sitting area. So she crawled across the floor to get the water and sat there drinking it, leaned up against the wall.

Liam walked out of the bathroom, saw her sitting there, and shook his head. "You don't listen, do you?"

"I needed water. I called for you, but you didn't hear me."

"And you couldn't have waited a few minutes for me to finish my phone call?"

"No. I was afraid I'd get nauseated again."

"I bet you were a handful as a child."

"Why do you think I'm an only child?"

He grunted. "My point exactly."

"You love me and you know it."

"Ha."

"Protest all you want, but I felt it last night."

"Simone, we don't have time to banter. Cranston is calling Webster-Reynolds for you about moving your meeting to this afternoon. I think you need to be seen by a walk-in clinic, if the hotel doesn't have a concierge doctor on staff. Some of the larger city hotels have those. I'm going to call down to the front desk and check. Can you stay put while I do that?"

"Yes. I'll sit right here and drink my water."

"You better, or I'll get my handcuffs out and chain you to the bed."

"Promises. Promises. But if you haven't noticed, there isn't a bedpost to use or a slot in the headboard to fasten them. You can't do it. Try again, Mr. Macho."

"You're sounding cheeky. You must be feeling a little better."

"Wrong again. My head is splitting. This is annoyance."

"Sexy annoyance."

"Now who is straying with the banter?" She cocked a brow at him.

He winked at her before going through the French doors into the bedroom. She heard him pick up the guest phone. A moment later he was speaking softly to whomever was on the other line.

She sipped the water and closed her eyes, really wishing she was back in the soft bed so she could go back to sleep. Curling up under warm covers right now sounded blissful. Snuggling up with Liam like she had last night wouldn't be bad either. Though that could be dangerous too. She might forget he was only comforting her and nothing more.

"We're in luck," Liam said.

She jumped, dropping the almost empty bottle of water.

"Sorry, didn't mean to startle you." He bent down and retrieved the bottle. "There is a doctor on staff who will be up to check on you shortly. I'm going to get you back in bed now."

"Do you think I should change?"

"No. Your pajamas are fine." He scooped her up and

carried her back into the bedroom, laying her on the bed. He even tucked her in, which she thought was nice.

"You gonna join me?"

He grinned. "No, I need to do some investigative work. I'm on the clock even if you aren't."

She pouted until he turned his back, and then she smirked. She watched him gather his clothes and head to the bathroom to change. Then she sighed, breathing in the smell of him on the pillow where she lay.

"Oh man, this is hard," she murmured.

She scooted over to her side of the bed where it was safer, even if the sun was shining through the open curtain. She attempted to sit up so she could close the curtain, but her head went spinning, so she laid back down and turned her back to it before falling asleep.

SOMETIME LATER SHE was awaken by a female doctor checking her vitals. "Hello, Simone. I'm Dr. Ballard. Your friend filled me in on what has been going on with you. As I understand it, this is the first time you've ever had a panic attack."

"Yes. I never passed out before either. Now I can't seem to sit up without getting dizzy or my head spinning. I also have a splitting headache."

"That's because your blood pressure is elevated due to the stress you are under. I'm going to prescribe a mild anti-anxiety pill for you to help you deal with this situation you are going through."

The doctor open up her bag and pulled out a prescription pad as well as a small rectangle box. "Here is a sample pack of the prescription to get you started today until you can get the prescription filled. Go ahead and take one."

Simone pushed herself to a sitting position and opened the box, pushing the pill through the aluminum backing, then reached for the unfinished bottle of water that Liam had left sitting on the bedside table.

"I recommend you rest today. Let your blood pressure return to normal. Eat a healthy diet of low sodium as well. I know being at a hotel it is not always that easy, but the menu here is pretty good. Also, while taking this medication avoid alcohol. Do you have any questions?"

"What if I can't rest this afternoon? I'm here on business and I had to move my morning meetings to this afternoon. I don't know if I can postpone them until tomorrow. I will try, but I don't know if my client will understand."

"Give me the name of your client and their fax number, and I will send them direct orders that you are on bed rest until tomorrow. I have no problem doing this. You have to get your blood pressure down, Simone. If you don't, you risk the possibility of having a heart attack or a stroke and you are too young to have damage from either one of those cripple your body for the remainder of your life."

"You're scaring me, Dr. Ballard."

"Good. Because this is serious. I highly recommend you follow up with your doctor immediately as soon as you return to Chicago. I've never seen anyone's blood pressure still be as high as yours was in their sleep after an episode. Liam estimated it had been a good twenty minutes since you passed out. It should have come down greatly during that time, but it didn't. I don't think you need a blood pressure medication. I believe this is all brought on by the stress of the situation you are going through. And until that is all put behind you I would continue taking this medication."

"Thank you."

"Now your client's name and fax number."

Simone gave her the information she needed.

"I recommend you order room service and eat something heart-healthy for breakfast. I'm also going to close these curtains a little more for you to help you rest."

"Yes, thank you," Simone said. "I couldn't get up earlier to do it myself and Liam was in the bathroom."

"Well it is taken care of now," Dr. Ballard said. She smiled. "I'll drop back by this afternoon or early evening to check on your blood pressure again. I want to monitor it the rest of the day, if you don't mind."

"That sounds fine."

"Then I'll leave you for now. Don't forget to eat healthy and drink plenty of water."

"I will do that," Simone said.

CHAPTER 11

LIAM ARRANGED with hotel security for one of their men to be stationed outside of the junior suite while he paid his old pal Sam Jensen a visit at Lincler Technologies & Securities. While Simone was sleeping that morning, he'd called Sam under the pretense that he was looking for a job in the DC area and they had a two o'clock appointment.

Sam met him at precisely two in the coffee shop on the plaza where the Lincler building was located. He was wearing a grey suit with a light blue dress shirt, no tie, and the top button undone. Liam had already ordered them coffee and had a table away from the other customers so they could talk in private.

"You could have knocked me over when I answered the phone this morning and it was you, Don Juan," Jensen said.

"Same here when I opened up the paper Monday on the Metro and there your name was in the article I was reading about Lincler Technologies & Securities."

They had a quick hug and then separated.

"So you are in DC looking for work you said? You've been cleared as one hundred percent after the explosion? Because if you are, I can get you in at Lincler easy. You can move up the ladder in the company and be a junior executive like me in no time."

Liam nodded. "Does Lincler have a problem with veterans?"

"No. Don't misunderstand me. They are all for hiring ex-military. They only want to make sure we have no mental issues. Some of our divisions deal in weapons and the last thing Lincler wants is someone that isn't all there opening fire and taking out the workforce, if you know what I mean."

"Yeah. I get your meaning." Liam got it loud and clear. "I've been cleared to return to work. I've even held a securities job for a few years, so I have references if that will help prove my stability. Like I said I've relocated and need a job now. I thought with you in town you might have a good idea who is and isn't hiring. I had an interview with one place, but when I went for it they had cleared out. Left the premises and didn't even notify me."

"That *is* strange. What business was that?"

"Testerman International."

Sam swallowed, then grinned, tapping the side of his coffee mug with his fingers. "Really?"

"I checked with the security guard at the building and he said that Testerman slipped out without anyone being the wiser. He also said that Lincler Properties owned the building. I made a call and sure enough Tawanda Ford, the building manager said that Lincler Properties and

Lincler Technologies and Securities is all one big conglomeration. Which supports what the security guard said about Lincler having its hands into everything. Would you say that's true?"

Jansen sat back in his chair and looked at him. "What are you really saying, Don Juan? This suddenly doesn't feel like you're here about a job. More like an investigation."

"I like to know whom I'm getting involved with before I take a job. If Helmand taught me anything, it's that life is too short. It can all be taken away in a flash. You have to be careful where you step."

"True. Lincler is a rising star. We want to be on top. We want to be the go to company in everything. That is part of our mission statement. There is nothing wrong with that. Maybe we'll be the next monopoly on the market. You can't hold that against us. If others have a problem with it that is just their issue, not ours."

"Fair enough." Liam took a sip of his coffee, then said, "Tell me more."

Jansen talked about the company for a while and then he invited Liam back to his office. He got him through security with a visitor's pass, which is what Liam was looking for all along. Once inside Lincler he could go snooping. It was a long shot not to get caught, but it was worth burning his tie with Jansen for Simone.

The problem was getting away from Jansen long enough to go snooping. It didn't look like that was going to happen.

"Want to take a tour of the facility?" Sam asked.

Liam shrugged. "Sure. Why not?"

He followed Sam to the bank of elevators and they went down to level G. "Main is M where we got on at plaza level. Floors one, two, and three are accounting, purchasing and the start of sales. I'm on four with the other junior executives as you already have seen," Sam explained.

When the doors opened they stepped out. "This is where shipping and receiving is located. Most new hires start down here to learn the ropes for the first few weeks. The CEO likes for us to get to know the company from the ground up."

"So you rotate through every department until you get to your final office?"

"Yes. That way you have a good hands on understand of the business to do your job better. It's a crash course really, but in the end it's worth the time and the money put into each employee. No one has ever said they regretted it. I know I didn't."

Liam nodded, mentally making note of his surroundings as they walked through the different areas and Sam talked about each division. At one point Sam stopped to talk to one of the foremen and Liam had a chance to wander off by himself to look over some of the equipment, but what he was really doing was seeing if there was a room off from that area that could have been the one Clayton Reid was held in for the video. Nothing looked familiar, and the noise level was clear that the kidnappers would not have done it during the day. Yet the lighting had been enough that even though the video was dim, there was a good source of light coming from somewhere.

"Sorry about that." Sam rejoined him. "Let's walk back to the elevators. The next floor up is G2 where shipping and receiving records are kept. The whole administrative division is stationed there. We'll stop for you to see."

"It looks to be a fine layout and a good foundation for a strong company," Liam said. "Can you point me to the men's room?"

"Of course. There's one right down from the bank of elevators here. I'll wait on you."

"Thanks. Too much coffee."

"I hear you."

Liam went into the men's room but when he came out again, he cautiously looked to see if Sam was watching for him. His old pal wasn't, having been caught once again by the same foreman. Liam took that opportunity to slip down the darkened corridor to investigate the far end of the basement area that wasn't in use.

There were several windowless doors, but each one was locked and as he turned the knobs he leaned against the steel door to see if he could hear anything on the other side. Nothing. If Clayton Reid was at Lincler, he wasn't in shipping and receiving.

Liam hurried back the men's room, pushed the door in and acted like he was just coming out when Sam finished his conversation.

"Ready to go?" Sam asked.

"Sure."

They stopped for a moment on G2, only for Liam to step off, look around, and get right back on the open elevator that Sam held with his hand. Then they went back up to the fourth floor and to Sam's office.

"I don't suppose you've seen enough to make you want to fill out an application to join Lincler have you?" Sam asked.

"It's tempting. Besides the application, what would I need to do?"

"There is a physical you'd have to pass. And since you were injured you'd have to have a psychological evaluation from your doctor to your mental state. I only know because I tried to get Billy Jennings on here a year or so ago and that is what he had to provide. He didn't get cleared."

"Billy Jennings wasn't even injured in Helmand, was he?" Liam asked.

"No. That was what I found so odd, but his psych eval was what kept him from being hired."

"How do you know so much of what went on in his hiring?"

"Billy told me why he didn't get hired." Sam stood. "If you'll excuse me, my coffee is begging to be released now."

"Sure man. Take your time."

Liam waited until the door closed behind Sam, and jumped up. He made fast work, sticking a small thumb drive into the USB port so he could copy data and do a search later. He quickly did a masking code to prevent anyone from Lincler's IT department from seeing that he'd been there and executed the command to copy the necessary files that he wanted onto the drive. When that was done, he pulled it out of the computer, put the thumb drive in a small compartment in the heel of his shoe, and ended the masking code. He was standing at the window, admiring the skyline when Sam walked back into the office.

"For the fourth floor, you sure do have a good view of DC."

"I know. I lucked up when I got this office. A straight-line view of the Washington Monument and the National Mall in the far distance, minus all the traffic in between."

"It's still a great view for a junior executive."

"So about that application?" Sam asked.

"Do I need to have my doctor at Walter Reed contact someone directly here in HR?"

"That would probably work just as well. Let me give you Nancy Handleman's business card. She handles hiring. I'll send her a reference for you myself and let her know you'll be submitting an application."

"Great." Liam took the card and slipped it into his pocket.

"It's really been great seeing you again. We should do dinner one night. I'd love for you to meet Danielle. She doesn't believe me when I talk about my days over in Helmand. But if she were to meet the great Don Juan, then maybe she would."

Liam grinned. "I'm not the great anything. I almost didn't come back from there and you know it. If I'd been smart, I wouldn't have been anywhere near that explosion. I'd have had insight and known it was coming."

"No one knew. We dealt with what we had and survived the best we could." Sam slapped him on the back. "Come on, I'll walk you back down. Here's my card as well. It has my cell number on it. Call me and we'll get together even if you don't get hired."

"You don't think I will?" Liam asked.

"I have no pull in these matters. So who knows?"

"I hear ya. Even if I don't, I'll give you a call."

They got on the elevator and went down to main. Sam waved to him as Liam walked to the security desk and returned his guest pass. Then he left the building. He walked a good block away before he placed a call to Hank Patterson.

"Hey, Hank, it's Liam Donovan."

"Hey, Liam, what's up? How's Chicago going? Hawkeye taking care of you guys?"

"Yes. But I'm in Washington DC right now on assignment. That's why I'm calling. Before you panic, I have no intention of leaving the Brotherhood Protectors, but I'm about to apply for a job. I'm doing this to get inside this organization for the assignment I'm on. I have no intention on doing that. I wanted to let you know before I did, because I'm sure they'll be calling you up asking questions about me."

"Gotcha, man. Anything I can do on my end?"

"I may need backup sent to DC if things play out the way I'm hoping. Brand, Wyatt, and Will are all tied up in Chicago."

"I can do that. Just send word and I'll have guys sent your way ASAP. Anything else?

"Watch out for Wyatt. He's on his way back there with a girl. They're going to Better Days. She was attacked and I know Wyatt is a great person to help anyone with PTSD, but if this girl is anything like her friend that I'm dealing with, he might be in over his head."

"You think so?" Hank said.

"I know so."

"Then I'll make a point of checking in with him, but I'm sure the folks at Better Days will be able to help him out if he needs it."

"He'll need reinforcements. Trust me."

"That bad?" Hank asked.

"Well, she does look sweet so maybe she isn't like my girl."

Hank chuckled. "You take care of your business and I'm sure Wyatt will do just fine. Talk to you later, Liam."

"Bye, Hank."

SIMONE WAS SITTING on the sofa painting her toe nails when he entered the junior suite. She looked his way and smiled. "Hi."

"How are you feeling? I thought you were supposed to be on bedrest?"

"I am resting. Painting my toenails is relaxing. If that guard out there would have allowed me to go down to the spa, I would have had a mani/pedi there, but he said I couldn't leave on your direct orders. So I had to cancel. He was nice enough to bring me my room service orders when they were delivered and remove the trays when I was finished."

"I couldn't risk you disobeying orders. Even for a mani/pedi."

"I know. Come sit down, kick off your shoes and I'll paint your toenails for you."

"Not on your life, sweetheart."

She pouted. "Oh, I thought I might catch you off guard

for a second. But seriously. Come sit down and tell me, did you have any luck finding my father?"

"I didn't. At least not yet. I'm going as far as applying for a job with this company I suspect could be involved so I can get access to the premises."

"Is that necessary?"

"I don't know. Maybe not. I'll turn in the application and let them start the vetting process on me at least. In the meantime, I'll sift through the data I collected while I was there today."

He got his computer out of his tactical bag and retrieved the thumb drive from the compartment in the heel of his shoe. It didn't take long for the thumb drive to bring up the information once he had the right program installed. He began searching for any information on Clayton Reid, Samwell Brady, or Testerman International. While the search was running, he got up and went to the little refrigerator to get a bottle of water.

"Do you want a bottle?" he asked Simone.

"Sure."

He started to toss it at her, but decided not to, because if she'd been painting her toenails she may have just finished her fingernails as well. He untwisted the bottle cap and handed one to her.

"Thank you."

"You're welcome." He took his bottle and sat back down as his laptop began making all sorts of beeping noises indicating matches

"Holy Moly!" Simone said. "Is your laptop going to explode?"

"No…I…I hope not."

She moved on the sofa so she could see the screen. "What is all that flashing? Wait. Is that my dad's name? And Samwell Brady? Even Testerman International?"

She looked up at him. "Liam, what have you found?"

"I've hit the jackpot. I've just tied Lincler, the company I met with today, to your father, Samwell Brady and Testerman International. Now, whether Lincler is behind your father's disappearance or not, I don't know. He sure wasn't there, at least as far as I was able to find, when I was given a tour of the facility. I'm hoping these files will tell me more so I have more proof."

"Jiminy." She sat back on the sofa and drank her water.

CHAPTER 12

NIGHT three in the junior suite

Simone lay on her side facing Liam, staring at him. He lay on his side, facing her as well. Neither of them said anything, and neither of them were sleeping. Time was ticking away like that on a bomb about to explode and yet neither of them could do anything about it. She'd still not been able to get a hold of her father's lawyer, which meant she couldn't get to the money for the ransom. Liam had gone through every file of data that he'd copied while at Lincler and was still no closer to proving that Lincler was involved in her father's kidnapping, even though his name and Samwell Brady's name were all over the files. Nor had he found any connection between Lincler and the gang from Chicago.

"What are we going to do?" she finally asked.

"I don't know." He turned onto his back and stared up at the ceiling. "Twenty-four hours is up and we haven't heard from the kidnappers. We should have hours ago.

They should have called, instructing you where the drop off point was if nothing else."

"But they didn't. Mom said they gave her two hours and when she refused to pay they sent her that video of me, making her think they'd shot me."

Simone sat up in bed. "Where's my phone?"

"Charging beside mine. Don't you remember? It hasn't made a sound."

"Are you sure it didn't power off? We'd better check it to be safe." Simone started crawling across the bed, but Liam reached over to the table next to him and grabbed her phone for her.

"Here. Take a look for yourself to settle your curiosity. It's on, but charging."

He was right of course. But that didn't stop her from checking the call log for any missed calls, or her message log to see if there was one that had come in without either of them noticing. She also turned up the volume on her phone so neither could sleep through it if they were to fall asleep.

"I think my father needs to find a new lawyer. One who will call back in a timely manner."

Liam grunted. "I'm sure he is making the big bucks. He can afford to make his clients wait."

"Unless he's not calling me back because he's involved." She said, leaning over him to lay her phone back on the table and reconnect the charger.

Liam grabbed her and before she knew it, he had her on her back. "What did you say?"

"What? What did I say?"

"About your father's lawyer?"

She blinked and thought for a moment. "That he might be involved in my father's disappearance and that is why he didn't call me back today."

Liam pushed himself up and off the bed. He began pacing the room like a caged tiger, running his fingers through his short cut, dark brown hair. "That's an angle I hadn't thought about. Who better to know about your father's finances than his own lawyer? What's his name again?"

"Stan Whittenbrier."

Liam went to the sitting room and got on his laptop. Simone followed, turning on a floor lamp for light.

"What are you doing?"

"I'm running a background on Mr. Whittenbrier to see what kind of dirt I can dig up on him."

"Do you always assume people are crooked?" she asked.

"In my line of work nine times out of ten they usually are, sweetheart."

"I'm not your sweetheart."

"If you say so."

She pursed her lips together and looked over his shoulder, ignoring his last comment. From what she was seeing, Whittenbrier was into plenty of unscrupulous dealings. She had to wonder if her father had any idea he was working with a man like that.

"You might as well run a background check on my father while you're at it. If you haven't already."

"I haven't. You said he wasn't into shady activity. What changed your mind?" Liam turned his head to glance at her.

"His kidnapping."

"If you're sure you want me to look into him?"

She swallowed, took a deep breath and then nodded. "Yes. I want you to do it. I have to know."

"Okay." He typed in the information required and ran the search on Clayton Reid.

Liam's laptop made a horrible noise and went black.

Simone jumped back. "Holy Moly!"

Then slowly there was white ticker tape writing of numbers and letters that began scrolling across the screen in a single row before large F. B. I. CLASSIFIED CONFIDENTIAL appeared.

"Did you know about this?"

"No," she squeaked. "What does it mean?"

"That either your father is an operative or he's been taken into custody."

"Into custody? For what?"

Liam shrugged. "I find it funny you assumed custody instead of him working for the F.B.I."

"Wouldn't he have told his family?"

Liam shrugged again. "Some agents don't, especially if they work undercover."

"It could explain why he was always keeping secrets from my mom."

"True."

"But why wouldn't he have told me?"

"To keep you safe? To keep you both safe."

Simone shook her head and walked over to the window in the suite, pushing back the sheers so she could get a better view of the city lit up at night. "I'm not sure which theory I prefer to believe about him. What if it is neither and he is a witness in protective custody? Couldn't that be a possibility?"

"You know what we're doing here? We're speculating. We have to remember that his information came up confidential for a reason. Why? I don't have clearance for. Brand would have clearance since he was a DEVGRU. I don't."

Simone turned away from the window. "Then we call Brand."

Liam shook his head. "We still have the threat from the kidnappers not to go to the authorities. I'm hesitant to involve anyone from the team in Chicago, unless I call Hawkeye. Since the deadline has passed and we still haven't heard from the kidnappers, I've almost ruled them out as a threat. But, I don't want to risk it either. We don't know if they haven't reached out because the FBI has swooped in and retrieved your father, or if they were trying to get someone else to pay the ransom and they hit the jackpot that way."

"Do you suppose they did?"

"It stands to reason they would. You heard your mother. They went to her first. Then to you. Why wouldn't they try someone else?"

"But who?"

"A possible girlfriend?"

"A girlfriend? My father? No way!"

"Simone, be realistic. Your father comes to DC. He stays at the Palomar Hotel. One of the trendiest hotels in the area where the younger demographic flock. I'd bet my bottom dollar that he has a younger girlfriend in the area."

"Yeah, but he's in his late fifties."

"Honey, men never are too old for a woman."

"Liam, you are talking about my dad."

"I am."

"I don't like thinking about my dad that way. Or my mom and Leland for that matter."

"So noted." He reached for her hand. "It's getting late. We better see if we can get some sleep now."

"Only if you put the barrier blanket back between us."

"Why?" He turned around, facing her. "I thought we'd gotten past that silliness."

"Silliness or not, you stay on your side. I stay on my side." She walked on toward the bedroom.

"Did I upset you by what I said about your dad? Is that why you want the blanket back?"

"No. I get it. But like you said, men are never too old for a woman. I don't want you forgetting our sleeping arrangements during the night."

"Oh, is that what you're afraid of? As I told you before, sweetheart, you have nothing to worry about. You aren't getting me in your bed that easy," he said.

Simone turned around and grinned, batting her eyes. "But sweetheart, I already have."

DAMN, *she had him there. And she looked so smug about it too.*

She started to crawl onto the bed and he cut her off by leaping into the middle of it.

"Liam!"

"Simone!" He playfully mocked her tone.

"You're on my side, now move."

"Maybe I want to sleep over here tonight." He clasped

his hands underneath his head, flexing his biceps to get her attention, but if she noticed, it wasn't obvious.

"Fine. I'll sleep on this side." She laid down with her back to him. "Good night."

He waited a few moments until he was certain she was settled and then he reached out and pulled her back toward him.

"Liam."

"Sorry, but I can't sleep. This worked last night for you. I thought it would work tonight for me."

"Really?" She twisted around, sitting up to look at him before flopping back down on the bed.

"Your pillow smells like your shampoo. I wanted to bury my face in your hair while I sleep."

"Say that again?" She slowly turned over to face him, running a finger up his chest and drawing a circle over the writing of his tattoo. "At least you're being honest. The real reason I wanted the blanket between us was so we had a barrier to keep me from you."

He silently groaned at her confession.

"Honey, you had me from the moment I walked into that bar Friday night."

"I did?"

He nodded.

"But I was a mess."

"A hot mess, screaming, 'I'm trouble! You better stay away!' But, I never was one to listen to warnings like that."

He pushed her hair away from her face, letting his finger trail down along her jawline before tilting her chin upward. Leaning forward, he kissed her gently, savoring the taste of her.

She ran her hand up his back and they rolled on the bed until he was covering her completely. The kiss deepened and she delved her tongue into his mouth as his darted into hers, their teeth clashed and they pulled apart, laughing.

"Whoa there, Rambo. Let me take the lead on this, okay?" Liam said. "Some things need to be taken slow."

"And some things need to happen now," she said huskily. She reached up and pulled his head back down to her, hungrily kissing him again.

He allowed her to win the kissing battle, but he was not about to let her win it all. He slowly worked to get her pajama bottoms off as they rolled back over so she was on top.

She broke free from their kiss long enough to come up for air, smiling down at him as she straddled him. With one hand, she pushed her hair back from her face. In another quick motion she had the tank off over her head, exposing her breasts for him.

He sucked in his breath, eager to get his hands on them, but he'd wait.

"What's the matter, Oklahoma?" she asked rising up on her knees so she could untie his lounging pajamas at the waist.

"Nothing. Are you a girl that likes to be on top?" He reached up to her hips and shimmied her panties down.

"Maybe."

He rose up to meet her in a sitting position. "And maybe I like you flat on your back under me. What do you say about that?"

She arched her brows. "Maybe I like that too."

He bent his index finger and moved it back and forth bidding her to come closer. She did and when she was within kissing distance, he pulled her closer and rolled them, so she was flat on her back, taking her underwear the rest of the way off in the process.

"That was a calculated move."

"Honey, you haven't seen nothing yet." He got up off the bed. "I'll be right back."

"Promises. Promises." Simone raised up on her elbows watching him walk away.

He hurried over to his suitcase, unzipped the side pocket where he kept his stash of condoms that he carried with him wherever the team went. He'd rather be prepared than SOL. Loverboy sure did find they came in handy. "Dammit."

"What?"

"I'm going to kill Will. He took the last condom from my bag and didn't tell me."

"Oh." The disappointment was clear in her voice. "Look in my bag. I usually have one or two in there. Just in case."

He glanced back at her. "Just in case?"

"Don't sound so surprised. Why do you carry them?"

"It's better to be safe than sorry."

"Exactly. I don't travel expecting to get laid. But if I meet someone and things progress, I do want to be prepared."

He unzipped her suitcase and found two glow in the dark purple neon packets. "Really? Glow in the dark?"

"Hey, Colleen bought them for Carly's thing last

Friday night. I snatched a few. I thought they'd be interesting conversation. Or a guiding light in the dark."

He chuckled, letting his pants fall to the floor before he crawled on the bed with her. "Any man with experience wouldn't need that to find his way around a beautiful woman's body."

"I don't let just any man around mine," she said, turning toward him as he lay down.

"Even if it is just casual?"

"Even if it is casual."

SHE TOOK the wrapper from him and tore it, unsealing the precious safety measure that would complete their tryst. "You know, I told Carly last Saturday I'd have little Donnie in my hands before the week was out. I don't think she really believed me."

"Little Donnie?" He laughed, shaking his head. "Simone, honey, you make lovemaking—"

"Sh-h-h." She put a finger up to his lips, cutting his words off. "Let's not call it that just yet. We're keeping it casual, remember."

There was a look that crossed his face for a split second that she couldn't ignore, but she didn't want to think about it at that moment. If she did, she'd be putting her clothes back on and going to sleep on the sofa. And maybe the smart thing was to do just that, but she never was one to listen to that little voice inside her head. Instead she handed him the open condom wrapper and began kissing his mouth, his neck.

His hands roamed her body, caressing and squeezing

in places that had her squirming and her nether regions strumming with liquid heat. He did magic with his mouth and hands on her breasts and, heaven above, what he did with his fingers before he ever entered her. He had her begging him to hurry and she forgot herself more than once, crying out his name as they rose to a climax and she shattered into pieces, while he soared on without her.

As the dawns light wafted through the window, they clung to one another and she trembled. Liam pulled the sheet up around their bodies before she finally drifted off to sleep, with her head laying on his chest listening to his heart still thumping from their lovemaking.

She may have wanted to have kept it casual between them, but what they'd just shared was anything but casual. The remarkable man lying with her had just rocked her world.

CHAPTER 13

SIMONE REACHED OUT A HAND, feeling for her phone to shut off the alarm, but instead she felt a nose and a mouth. She opened one eye and snorted, seeing Liam glaring at her.

"Not funny, sweetheart."

"Sorry." She rose up and turned off the alarm, then snuggled closer to Liam. "Tell me I don't have to get up and go to meetings today."

"You don't have to do anything you don't want to do, but stay right here beside me."

"That sounds like you want me to lose my job."

"No. I was telling you what you asked me to tell you. With a little extra thrown in."

She ran her index finger around one of his areolas until it was a hard bead and he gave a throaty groan.

"Are you looking for trouble this morning?" he asked her.

"Always. Too bad I don't have time to finish what I started." She raised up and kissed him lightly, but he wrapped his arms around her and rolled, pinning her onto the bed with his body.

He stared down at her with hunger in his eyes. "You should never start something you don't have time to finish, sweetheart."

"Can I take a raincheck for later?" She slowly ran her foot up the back of his calf.

"That can be arranged. But how about I join you for your shower?"

She grinned. "I don't think that would work. We'd end up doing other things besides showering."

"I know." He dipped his head to her neck and began kissing her there before moving behind her ears. "So maybe we should just skip the shower part and stay right here?"

"As much as I'd like that, I have my meetings from yesterday with Webster-Reynolds this morning. It's going to be hard enough after last night without having me overheated from your kisses."

"True. Just remember, you started it." He moved away, sounding cool, so she could get up and go.

She hurried from the room after grabbing a bra and a panty from her suitcase. His tone lingered with her though, just like that look he'd given her last night before they'd made love... Had sex... Dammit, now he had her calling it what it shouldn't have been because she had wanted to keep it casual, but it had turned into more. Why did guys always react that way when a girl wanted to be casual about sex? Wasn't that normally what most of them wanted? She just didn't get the double standard in this modern age.

She quickly pinned her hair up to keep it from getting wet before she jumped into the shower. Standing under the spray, she lathered and rinsed before turning the water off.

The shower curtain scraped back a small distance and a fluffy towel came toward her.

"Thanks, Liam." She started drying off, getting her arms, her legs, and her back in quick fashion. "Should I turn the water back on for you?"

"I'll give you time to finish in here before I get in. You have a phone call."

"I do?"

"Your dad's lawyer's office."

"Finally!" She wrapped the towel around her and hopped out.

"I left your phone by the bed."

"Okay."

Running out of the bathroom, she went around the corner, through the open French doors into the bedroom. Sitting down on the bed, she picked up her cellphone. "Hello, this is Simone."

"Miss Reid, this is Phoebe Dandridge. We spoke briefly Monday afternoon."

"Yes, I remember. I told you I needed to speak to Mr. Whittenbrier immediately that it was a matter of life and death and you said he'd return my call the next day. He still hasn't returned my call, by the way."

"That is why I'm calling you. I feel terrible about that. He usually checks in, but he didn't, which is highly irregular," Phoebe's voice broke off and she sounded like she was crying. "I'm sorry, please forgive me, but I thought you should know that Mr. Whittenbrier will not be getting in touch with you because he was found...he was found floating in the Chicago River."

"Oh my God. I'm so sorry. Oh, you poor woman. Where?"

"Southbank, near the river walk. It's close to our offices. He always liked to walk there after leaving work in the evenings. An investigation has been opened up. I really don't know anymore, but if you are needing his services you'll want to be speaking to another attorney here at Whittenbrier and Lambert."

"Thank you. I will call back if I do need further assistance. I appreciate it." She hung up the call and looked at Liam, standing in the doorway, wearing his lounging pants.

"What was that about?"

"Whittenbrier is dead. His body was found in the Southbank of the Chicago River near his office building. That's the reason he hasn't returned my call."

"Damn. That throws a wrench in my theory that he was behind this. I'm calling Hawkeye to see what he can tell me about his murder."

"You'll keep me posted throughout the day on what you find?" She went to the closet and pulled out an outfit before going back to the bathroom.

"Sure."

Liam's tone made her feel like she had already lost his interest. He was preoccupied with the murder of Whittenbrier and how that possibly fit in with her father's kidnapping or not. So be it.

She finished getting ready, gathered her things and left

for Webster-Reynolds within half an hour, telling him she'd see him later. Whether he heard her or not, he didn't acknowledge her.

The metro was crowded and she was lucky to squeeze into the car she got on without having to wait for the next one.

"Would you like my seat?" a young lawyer type asked. "I think I can handle the jerks and stops better than you in those shoes you're wearing."

Simone glanced down and noticed she'd put on the wrong heels for work. In her haste to get out the door, she'd slipped on the evening pumps instead of the business heels she'd brought. "Thank you."

He stood and as he moved away from the seat, she stepped forward before someone decided to be rude sit down in her place.

"Out of towner?" the young man asked.

"That obvious?"

He held up his hand, positioning his index finger and thumb a small distance apart. "Just a fraction."

"I'm on business. Running late, as usual, this week because my normal hotel had to reassign me three blocks away from where I work."

"I'm on business too, but I come every other week so I feel like a regular these days. I asked my employer if I shouldn't just move here and save them on travel expenses, but they said living expenses and moving would come to more than the travel."

Simone nodded as the tram slowed for her stop. "This is me. I thank you for the seat and the conversation. It took my mind off of my morning."

"It's my stop too. Care to walk together?"

"I might slow you down in these heels," she warned, not certain she liked the idea of having him tag along with her. He seemed nice enough and walking down the street to their different destinations couldn't really hurt anything. For all she knew he could be going in one direction and she could be going in another when they reached street level.

"I don't mind. I'm an hour early as it is anyway."

Great. Just my luck that I can't get rid of him because he is an early bird.

"Lead the way then," she said.

They walked through the turnstile and followed the flow of traffic outside into the morning sunshine. She headed toward the streetlight at the corner and so did he. There was nothing she could do, but smile. They crossed with the other pedestrians when the walk signal lit up and she headed straight down the block. At the next corner, they were stopped by another light.

"I'm going right here," he said. "No chance you do as well?"

"Afraid not, I go straight."

"Maybe we'll run into each other again tomorrow morning?"

"We might."

"I'm Douglas, by the way."

"Simone."

"Have a great day, Simone."

"You too, Douglas."

When the signal turned for him to go his way, she felt relief yet foolish. He was just being a nice guy. Still she'd become all apprehensive because he'd wanted to walk with her, which as a single female she should be because one could never be too cautious.

The signal finally turned for her to cross the street. On the other side, she passed a few store fronts and went into the coffee shop where she had been stopping every morning before going into Webster-Reynolds. It was her normal routine.

The girl at the counter smiled, nodded, and asked. "Do you want your usual?"

"Yes, please."

She rang her up, while the barista started on her java.

Simone dug out her money from her bag and paid, picked up the steaming beverage, and headed out the door. She'd gotten two doors down when a nondescript white service van pulled out of an alleyway, blocking her progression. The side door opened and two men dressed in all black jumped out and grabbed her, making her drop her java, and threw her inside. Jumping in after her, they slammed the door back and the van sped away.

CHAPTER 14

Simone fought against the men, kicking and elbowing. "You made me drop my coffee and I lost a shoe, you creeps! Let me go!"

"Shut up."

The voice sounded familiar. *Douglas?*

She knew she shouldn't have walked with him, seemingly nice or not. Look where it had landed her. And why? What good would abducting her do them? She was upset her and she wasn't about to sit still like a docile rag doll.

She kicked one of the masked men in the groin. He doubled over, cursing. The other, whom she assumed was Douglas, if that really was his name, came after her, but she elbowed him in the gut and did a backward fist pop to his mouth and nose.

"Get her tied up and gagged. What's taking you so long back there?" the driver of the van inquired.

"She's not making it easy," the bent over guy panted.

Simone scrambled away from Douglas, trying to get to the side van door. Her objective was to reach it by the time the van got stopped at the next light so she could jump out and get lost in the throng of pedestrians. With one pump that wasn't going to be easy, but she'd lose it too if it made running easier. Maybe she'd get lucky and there would be a cab behind the van that she could easily jump into and it could speed away down a side street. Taxi drivers knew all the shortcuts in a city. So as farfetched as it sounded, it could happen and work out for her.

She'd reached the door, but bent-over-guy had recovered enough to leap toward her before she got the door open. He pulled her backwards and held her arms behind her back while Douglas secured her wrists with what felt like hard plastic. Then he slapped a wide piece of gray duct tape over her mouth.

"That should keep you quiet."

She glared at him.

"Too bad things had to work out this way for you, Simone. I think we could have enjoyed riding the metro together."

She felt a small prick at her arm and turned her head in time to catch the other guy removing a needle from her arm. What had he given her? Whatever it was it sure had a potency. She immediately felt drowsy. Her eyes started fluttering and she slumped over against the guy.

SIMONE OPENED HER EYES SLOWLY, feeling groggy. Her eyes fluttered closed and then opened again. She blinked several times trying to wake fully, not recognizing where she was with each small glimpse of the dark room she was in. Had they had to change hotel rooms again and she forgot? Her new anxiety medicine was having a strange effect on her.

Liam.

She tried to speak, but no sound came out. Or had it? She couldn't tell. She felt like she was down a well or a long tunnel.

"Simone! Simone! Are you awake, honey? It's your father."

"Daddy. Oh, Daddy. I lost you and couldn't find you." She imagined she was a little girl skipping in the yard at their house to him and he caught her in his arms hugging her tight.

"Oh baby. I'm so sorry this had to happen to you. I told them to leave you alone, that you knew nothing, but they wouldn't listen."

Simone blinked, inhaling her father's scent. She clung to him tightly as her senses came fully awake. Then she slowly pulled away, looking at him, fully taking him in.

"Oh my God, it really is you. How? Wh-what is going on?"

"It's a long story, honey."

"One I think you need to tell me, don't you?" She looked around the dark room, taking in her surroundings. The room looked very much like the one her father had been in on the video that was sent during the ransom demand. She looked down and saw she was sitting on a full mattress set. She cleared her throat and coughed, then leaned closer to him so she could speak softer. "And you can start by explaining why your background is classified confidential with the FBI."

Her father was silent for several minutes, just looking at her, before he finally said, "How the hell did you find that out?"

"Like you, I have my secrets."

He shook his head. "You were snooping around. That's why they grabbed you."

"I thought it was because I didn't pay the one million dollar ransom like they wanted. But I couldn't get to the money. I called Whittenbrier on Monday to get the power of attorney changed so I could get access like you always told me if something should happen to you, but he was out of the office. I called again on Tuesday without any luck either. I never heard back about paying the ransom. Which was so strange. Then his assistant called this morning. Whittenbrier is dead."

Her dad nodded. "Doesn't surprise me. I told them you couldn't get to my money without going to him. They must have grabbed him instead and he couldn't give it up."

"Are you sure he wasn't involved? He's got a shady file, dad. His background... you need to be more careful who you pick for an attorney in the future."

"Simone, where are you getting this information?"

"I have my sources. You just tell me what I need to know about how you got here. What did you do? Why did I have a gang member point a gun at me but there was no bullet when he pulled the trigger? Your kidnappers got video of it and sent this to mom after she wouldn't pay the five million they demanded in ransom for you. They made her think that I had been killed."

"I've seen the video, Simone. They used that same video to lure me to an isolated location so they could abduct me. But then they showed me a clip of you and your friend Carly going into Chicago Med the next day once I got here so I knew you were okay."

"They what?!" Simone jumped up off the mattress, but her legs felt like jelly and she was right back down on it in a matter of seconds. "Oh, that wasn't a smart move. I don't know what kind of shot they gave me, but it was a doozy."

"It's best if you sit still, try to stay calm."

"What do these people want?" she asked.

"Retribution. I sold some bad weapons to them. Military grade that I got from a company I deal with on a regular basis."

"Let me guess, Lincler Technologies and Securities?"

"How do you know that?"

"Again, my source."

"Are you sure you don't have something you need to tell me, little girl? Have you switched from sales with Robert Cranston and gone into undercover work?"

She grinned. "I'm still working for Cranston. In fact I'm in DC for the second week making up where I flubbed up the first week with a client because I spent too much time searching for you. So Cranston sent me back. Now I've been abducted, but at least I've found you this time."

She leaned in and hugged him and he hugged her back. "I just hope that mom and Leland are safe at the Willard and they aren't found in DC and end up getting abducted too."

"You mom and Leland are coming to the city? Why?" Her dad released her.

"Because mom was frantic to see me after that video

the kidnappers sent. She wouldn't listen to reason that I was fine and they were on the next flight out."

"That is so Gloria. Surely Leland can keep her safe while they are here."

Simone looked by the mattress set for her purse or computer bag. "They took my bags. If mom calls my cell they'll find out she's in town."

"They might just turn the phone off."

"I hope not. The GPS tracker will help Liam locate us if he finds out I didn't show up at Webster-Reynolds."

"Who is Liam?" Clayton asked.

Simone felt her cheeks warm and she was smiling in spite of herself at the way her father asked that question.

"He's my source."

"Tell me about him."

"What do you want to know?"

"For starters how does Liam have access to all this information?"

She leaned closer to him. "This room isn't bugged, is it?"

"I don't know. I haven't had anyone to talk to the whole time I've been here."

"I can trust you, daddy. Right? You aren't really with these guys."

"Simone! Why would you even ask a question like that?"

She sat back away from him and swallowed. "It's hard to know who to trust after you've been shot at, and abducted off the street. And find out that your father has been keeping secrets from you all of his life. And still hasn't explained why his file is classified confidential."

"Which this Liam person has access to, so he is obviously someone you trust more than me right now." Her dad looked hurt, like he was losing her. "I get it, kiddo."

"My life has been turned upside down, daddy. I've been prescribed anti-anxiety medication because of it. I've been having panic attacks. Too much to deal with."

"I'm sorry, honey, but the truth is I don't know why my background is marked classified confidential with the FBI. Maybe your friend Liam pulled up the wrong profile."

"It was the right one. I gave him your date of birth, mother's maiden name. He wasn't just putting in a name and state to do the search."

"Well, who knows then? Maybe I'm a wanted man. And once I get out of this, the FBI might come knocking at my door."

"Don't be glib about it. This is serious."

"First things first though, this Liam guy. Who is he?"

Simone explained about Liam and how he came to be assigned to her after the shooting at the bar, and how he'd helped her get past her meltdown once they'd gotten back to her apartment that night.

"He came to DC with you?"

"Yes."

"Sharing the same hotel room?"

"Yes, but only because the connecting rooms at the hotel I booked didn't get transferred when we were reassigned at the last minute. But we're making it work."

"I don't like it."

"Daddy, it's not like I'm a virgin. You knew that."

"I still don't like it, Simone. He's a stranger."

"Not anymore."

"Simone!"

"Well. You know me and a good looking man. If I set my eye on him I'm going to find a way to get him…"

Clayton shook his head, holding up a hand to stop her from speaking. "Don't say more. I don't want to have images of the two of you together in my head when I meet him…if I meet him."

"Oh, you'll meet him," Simone said. "We just have to figure out a way to get out of here."

CHAPTER 15

Liam hung up the phone with Hawkeye, stood up and stretched. He packed up his laptop and hung his tactical bag on his shoulder before he headed out of the hotel suite. He wasn't sure where he'd go, but he needed to get out of there so the maid service could come in and clean.

Stepping off the elevator at lobby level, his cell rang. It was Hawkeye calling him back.

"Hey, did you find something out already?" Liam asked, walking over to a sitting area in the atrium of the hotel.

"No. I just got off the phone with a Robert Cranston. He said he is Simone Reid's boss here in Chicago. He'd received a call from Webster-Reynolds there in DC, the client she was supposed to have met with this morning. She never showed. Cranston has been trying to reach Simone on her cell all morning, but it goes to voice mail. Since the man didn't have your number he called here and the switchboard put him through to me."

"Damn. I've screwed up…She left for work hours ago.

We've been on and off the phone since she left, working on putting pieces together with Whittenbrier and Lincler. Simone could be anywhere in the DC area or halfway across the US by now if they put her on a flight."

"Liam—"

"I've screwed up big time here. I should have gone with her this morning."

"Liam—"

"After we got the ransom demand on her father, I should have had the forethought to have realized she could have been next."

"Liam! Listen. You can't blame yourself. You have been with her twenty-four seven. You are one man. While she took care of business you were trying to track down her father for her."

"But I should have taken her to work today. Why didn't I realize that? Instead I was too preoccupied with Whittenbrier's death to pay much attention to when she left. I don't even recall what she was wearing. I can't give a detailed description if I'm asked. What kind of a protector am I? I let her get abducted because I...got too close."

"What happened?"

"I slept with her."

"You did?"

"Yeah. I slept with her. Brand told me to remember she was my assignment, not my date, but I threw caution to the wind and forgot all of that. If he finds out, I'm sure I'll be off his team."

"We're men, Liam. Brand is one, too. I'm sure he'll understand if he finds out. But the only way he'll know is if you tell him."

"He always knows when we screw up."

"Well, for the record I want you on my Chicago Protection Task Force, so it doesn't matter what Brand says. Do you want to work for me or not?"

"Sure."

"Then it is settled. If he gives you flack, he'll have to answer to me."

There was a brief pause on the line before Hawkeye said, "Now, about Simone. You'll need back up."

"Yeah. I will, but I think Hank has provided that already. I spoke to him yesterday about sending someone if I needed it, but I never dreamed he'd show up with another Brotherhood Protector today. They just walked into the hotel here."

"How'd they find you so easy?"

"GPS tracker on my phone. I better go talk to them. I'll keep you informed." Liam ended the call, still not believing that Hank had gone ahead and traveled all this way with Alex "Taz" Davila.

Taz was like him. He'd had a traumatic brain injury after an IED explosion and, after his rehabilitation, was tagged by Leigha Nipton as potential Brotherhood material. Hank Patterson had approved and the rest was history. Taz went on to work at the Better Days Ranch on assignment where he met his wife, Hannah Kendricks.

Liam walked to the middle of the lobby and greeted them. "Man. You guys showing up here is perfect timing."

"I was afraid after we spoke yesterday you'd be needing help faster than a team could get here, so Taz and I talked and decided to jump on the next available flight." Hank explained. "What's happened?"

"Simone, the girl I've been assigned to protect, never showed up for a meeting with a client this morning. I was just notified thru Chicago PD when her boss got word to them, trying to reach me."

"Okay. So what can we do?" Taz asked.

"Track her cellphone via GPS to see if we get a location while gathering intel from local CCT spots around town."

"Let's see if we can get a room and get set up in it." Hank said. "If not, we'll go to yours, Donovan."

"Sure."

Hank spoke to the manager at the front desk and the next thing Liam knew, they were headed upstairs to the second floor to a small conference room where they set up their equipment. Liam started a GPS search on Simone's phone, while Taz worked on connecting to the local CIT towers.

Half an hour later, room service arrived with food that Liam didn't realize Hank had ordered for them. But he'd gotten burger and fries for the three of them along with iced tea. They ate while they worked.

"I'm having no luck pinging Simone's phone. It must be turned off."

"Come look at this. I think I finally found the footage we want. Here is the metro line right before eight a.m.," Taz said. "Do you see her in the crowd?"

Liam came and stood behind him, watching the poor quality color stream of people coming out of the metro station. "There she is. See her red hair shining in the sunlight?"

"If you say so." Hank leaned in closer. "Is she talking to the guy to her right?"

"Can you slow the footage down, Taz?" Liam asked.

"Sure. I can even back it up if you want a replay of the last few seconds."

"Do that so I can see it again. I need to see if she was really talking to the guy on her right."

Liam watched closely. Simone glanced at the guy to her right. She did speak to him and he was definitely saying something to her. They even walked in the same direction and together for a good distance before they parted ways.

"Does she know anyone in town that you know about?" Hank asked.

"Not that she has mentioned to me."

"Taz, can you get a good close up of that guys face so we can run a facial recognition on him."

Liam turned away for a moment, placing his hands on the back of one of the table chairs and thought about this. He didn't want to jump to conclusions. It could have been a friendly conversation for all he knew. Maybe someone she sees on the metro every morning. But it still irked him that she'd be so careless in a city this size when her father is already missing. Not to mention after they'd just spent the night together.

He tamped that emotion down. He couldn't go there. She'd said she wanted to keep things between them casual. Maybe she could do that, but not him. Not after the way they'd come together and everything had exploded. It was like they'd bared their souls to one another and he wasn't usually the type to get all gushy and sentimental over a sexual encounter with a woman like Simone, but something was definitely different with her. He'd picked up on it from the moment he'd walked into the Pied Piper.

"Hey Liam, look at this."

"What is it?" He turned back to the laptop monitor and saw Simone coming out of a coffee shop and walking down the street when a white, nondescript van came out of an ally way. It stopped, blocking her path. The side door opened. Two men jumped out, grabbed her and pulled her into the van.

"No!" He gripped the back of the chair tight.

"This is good. We know what happened. Now we have to figure out where they took her. We're gonna see if we can't track that white van. You keep trying to ping her cell while I run facial recognition on the guy she was walking with on the street."

Hank grasped him on his shoulder and squeezed. "This really narrows our search down. It may feel like the end of the world, but it isn't."

"We have to get her back, for so many reasons."

"I understand. One being she's yours, am I right?" Hank said.

Liam blinked. "How?"

"I'm your leader. I know things."

"Just like Brand always knows." Liam shook his head.

"That's right. Besides, her red hair wasn't glowing. That was a dead giveaway to me that she meant something to you," Hank added.

"Oh yeah," Taz agreed. "Dead giveaway."

Liam grimaced, going back to his laptop to sit down

and ping Simone's cellphone number again. This time he got a hit, and he followed the cell towers in the city trying to triangulate a location.

"I got a hit," he announced.

"I got a facial recognition," Hank said a moment later. "And I think you will want to come see this one, Liam."

He jumped up and went over to where Hank sat. The elation he felt drained from his body when he saw Sam Jensen's military picture on Hanks' screen as the match to the guy Simone had been talking to on the street.

He tore out of the conference room with both Hank and Taz calling after him. Hank caught up with him by the elevator as he passed back and forth waiting for one to come.

"Where do you think you're going?" he demanded.

"Lincler, to beat the shit out of Jensen."

"No you aren't."

"Watch me."

"Don't make me fire your ass, Donovan. I'm ordering you to stand down immediately. You going off halfcocked is not going to get Simone or her father back here any quicker. We need to strategize. Come back into the conference room and let's talk things through before we go out there unprepared."

It took Hank half an hour to convince Liam that his plan of action was the right one to take. And another half hour of talking with the DC metro police chief to get him on board with what their plans were. Liam, Hank, and Taz left the Hamilton with their gear and were picked up by an unmarked, DC metro car.

"Here are the directions of the location," Hank handed the driver the information on a piece of paper.

"Gotcha. I'll go ahead and give these coordinates to our SWAT team who are on standby. They'll be in the area waiting for our go ahead once we check the place out. If it turns out to be a bust, they won't move in."

"Sounds great," Hank said.

"Once we get Simone, then we can hit Lincler," Liam said.

"You won't have to do that," the driver said.

"Why's that?" Taz asked.

"The FBI raided them this morning. Shut the whole facility down."

Liam hit the back of the front passenger seat with the palm of his hand. "I knew that company was bad news. Can you drive a little faster?"

The man pulled out his siren, reaching through the window to stick it on the roof of the car before speeding through traffic, weaving in and out of lanes faster than most New York taxi drivers that Liam had seen. He just prayed that they reached Simone before the kidnappers got antsy and decided to move for good measure.

SIMONE LAY ON THE BED, staring up at the ceiling, resting. Her dad was across the room somewhere, doing whatever he had been to preoccupy himself since he was taken. He still hadn't told her the whole story. He'd attempted to tell her, but she knew what bits and pieces he'd shared had plenty of holes in it like Swiss cheese.

"Dad, are you still there?" she asked.

"Yes, where else would I be?"

"Just checking that they didn't come and take you away while I was spaced out," she said.

"No, they didn't."

"I'd get up and walk around the room, but my legs still feel like jelly."

"That is odd."

"Is there a bathroom?"

"Yes. Over here."

Clayton came out of the shadows and helped her walk the short distance to the tiny bathroom that actually had a shower. The light was dim, but it was okay. There was a shelf with towels and wash cloths. Toiletries, including an electric razor. No wonder her dad had not looked bad in the video.

"I think I can manage. Thanks." She held onto the wall for support until he closed the door, then she lifted the soft eyelet, cold shoulder dress to her waist, glad she'd decided on it instead of the suit today. It was far more comfortable to be captured in that a suit. She removed her hose while she sat on the commode. There was no point wearing them any longer. Her pumps were gone.

She finished up in the bathroom, washed and dried her hands before she opened the bathroom door. Voices greeted her, so she stopped and slowly inched the door back shut.

Leaning against the door, heart pounding, she felt ill for a second. She slowed her breathing the best she could, taking deep, calming breaths, in and out, until she felt more in control of the situation. Then she gently pulled back on the door to see if she could tell who was out there with her father. Was it the men in black who had kidnapped her?

Before she could get a good look, the door was kicked open and she was pulled out into the main room with her father by one of the masked men.

"No hiding," he said.

"I wasn't hiding." She defended herself.

"We're leaving. Let's go."

No! No! They couldn't go. What if Liam had tracked them down? What if he was on his way to wherever this place was to find them? Think, Simone, think. How can you stall this move?

She clutched her stomach. "I don't feel good. I think I'm going to be sick."

"That's right. She's been ill ever since she came around. Whatever you gave her has made her ill," Clayton said.

"We'll get you a barf bag for the ride. Let's go." The guy grabbed her arm and jerked her along behind him as they started down a hallway.

"Hey now, no rough handling." Clayton tried stopping him.

The guy stopped, pulled a gun from his waistband and pointed it at him. "You watch yourself old man. I'm not afraid to use this on you or her. I don't care if the rest of them believe you are a cash cow. I see you as nothing but trouble."

"Then let us go." Simone looked him straight in the eye showing him she wasn't afraid.

The guy looked back at her for several heart beats before he finally shook his head. "I can't do that."

"Ah, then you're not in control of this operation."

Simone felt she was walking on dangerous ground trying to bait him, but it was worth a shot to get it to slow their move from this location. For some reason she had a strong feeling that Liam was on his way. Maybe it was only wishful thinking, but she knew they didn't need to leave here.

"No more talking."

The guy was getting testy, so she had hit a nerve. That was good. Now for her next move, but what? What could she say to make him falter further down the rabbit hole? Maybe she didn't have to say anything. After all he was pulling her along. All she needed to do was pretend a trip or a stumble and fake a sprained ankle. That would put a halt on things for a few moments.

She did a perfect move, tripping up the last step, yelping out in pain at the exact moment Liam and his team burst through the double stairwell doors and met them on the loading dock landing.

The two men with Liam had the gunman, removed the gun from him and were leading him away in no time. Simone was so glad to see Liam, but she remembered how he'd ignored her this morning before she left the hotel room.

"It took you long enough," she told him.

"Sweetheart, you're not an easy woman to track down. Which is good, because I'm always up for a challenge."

He had her grinning at him with that line, and she knew she was so far gone it was pathetic.

Her dad cleared his throat and she looked at him, having forgotten he was there.

"Liam, my father, Clayton Reid. Daddy, Liam 'Don Juan' Donovan, the man I'm crazy about."

"Is that so, Sweetheart?" Liam said.

Simone nodded, stepping toward him and wrapping her arms around his neck. "You know it is. Now shut up and kiss me."

Liam looked at her dad. "It's nice to meet you, Mr. Reid. Do I have your permission to do as she asks?"

Her dad chuckled. "He's polite. I'll give him that. Proceed son, before she gets surly."

"Yes, sir. Thank you, sir."

CHAPTER 16

THE DC METRO PD CHIEF wanted both Simone and her father be taken to the nearest hospital to be checked out. However, Hank Patterson convinced him that neither looked to be suffering from their abduction, and if the EMT who checked them over didn't think they needed additional care, then they should leave it at that.

"It's your call, but if either have issues down the road, it will be on you for not letting them be seen."

"I hear you chief. I hear you." Hank signed the refusal for treatment form, as well as Simone and her father, before they left the Lincler property where they'd been held.

"I'm going to take off, honey," Clayton said, giving Simone a hug.

"What do you mean? No, you aren't leaving. You still have some answering to do."

"I've told you everything I can, Simone. Don't make me lie to you like I had your mother all those years ago."

Simone tilted her head to the side and gave her father and long look. "Oh, daddy. Why didn't you ever tell her the truth?"

"It was safer that way. And that is all I am saying now. It is safer this way."

"Your luggage is still at the Palomar, sir." Liam reached out his hand for him to shake.

"You take care of my Simone. She's my most valuable asset."

"That I will."

Simone hugged her dad tight, then kissed him on the cheek. "Be nice to Edna. She deserves a special something when you return."

"Of course she'll get something special. She always does. She's my Rock of Gibraltar. I couldn't manage without her. I'll be in touch, kiddo."

They watched as he walked away. As Simone wiped a tear from her eye, she turned to Liam and hugged him.

One of the men who had been with Liam earlier when he'd burst through the door came over carrying her purse and laptop bag. "I believe these belong to you. They were found in the white van inside the building there."

"Thank you! Thank you." Simone took both, sitting the laptop bag down. She dug into her purse looking for her cellphone. She had several missed calls from Robert Cranston and even more calls from her mother.

"I bet I've lost my job," she said.

"No. Cranston was trying to reach you, but when he couldn't he called Hawkeye who then contacted me."

"I know, but I promised him I'd follow through and

not let my dad's disappearance get in the way of me doing my job and I have. Without meaning to, I have."

"Things happen. If your boss can't understand that, then maybe that isn't the job for you."

She looked at the man not sure what to say.

"Simone, meet Alex 'Taz' Davila from the Brotherhood Protectors. He flew all the way out here with Hank Patterson today after I spoke to Hank yesterday because they wanted me to have backup when I needed it."

"We arrived just in time, too," Taz said.

"Thanks for coming," Simone said. "I really appreciate your assistance and everything you and the Brotherhood Protectors stand for. Plus, your service you gave for our country."

"Thanks. You're welcome anytime out at Better Days if Liam ever decides to come back to Montana. I'd better go find Hank. He was checking on a flight back tonight. It would be great to get back there and sleep in my own bed. If you'll excuse me."

"What does he mean, if you ever go back to Montana?" Simone asked.

"I've been offered a job in Chicago working for Hawk-eye's new Chicago Protection Task Force if I want it. I guess it really depends on if you want me to stick around."

She smiled. "Of course I want you to stick around. If you want to stick around."

He scooped her up in his arms, grabbing her laptop bag in the process. "Let's get you off this nasty pavement. Hank and Taz are waving at me to come on. It looks like they're ready to head back to the hotel."

· · ·

SIMONE CALLED Robert Cranston as soon as she got back to the hotel suite to let him know she was safe. "I'm sorry this happened. I know I told you that nothing would get in the way of me fulfilling my obligation to Webster-Reynolds on this trip, but I never anticipated getting abducted on the street before I walked into their building. I'm fully willing to resign my position as soon as I return to Chicago."

"Simone, stop right there. One of Webster-Reynolds employees saw the abduction and reported it to Webster. When I spoke with Webster today I told him about your father being abducted and how you'd receive a ransom demand, had health issues from it, but was still willing to meet with him, only to be abducted yourself. Webster said he is satisfied with the time you have spent with them this week and last. He doesn't expect you to come in tomorrow. You can come back to Chicago Friday as planned. Enjoy the extra day to relax if you like."

"Wow. This is not what I had anticipated. Thank you! Thank you very much for understanding, Mr. Cranston. I'll be back in the office on Monday."

"Yes you will. Have a good weekend, Simone."

She smiled, scooting back on the bed, so that she leaned back against a few pillows stacked in front of the headboard before she called her mom.

"Simone! Oh darling, I have wonderful news. Your father called. He is fine. Said he has been out of the country on business for several weeks and just wanted to check in with us to make sure everything is going well."

"He did?" Simone shook her head. *Oh daddy!*

"So that whole ransom thing was a horrible cruel scam. But I still do not know how they got that footage of you."

"I don't either, Mom. So are you and Leland here in DC already?

"Yes. We're at the Willard. Why don't we have dinner tonight?"

"How about tomorrow instead? I have a headache and want to turn in early. I'll probably just order in something."

"Then I won't keep you. Have a good early night."

"Night."

Simone put her phone on the night stand, slipped off the bed and went to her suitcase to get a night gown and a pair of panties before she jumped in the shower. She scrubbed her hair and body clean, but she still didn't feel okay. She imagined that must be a fraction of what Colleen was feeling like these days. She brushed and blew her hair dry, making sure it was fully tangle free and dry before she left the bathroom and crawled in bed.

Liam had not come up from the conference room where he'd stopped with Hank and Taz, but that was okay. She needed to rest and if he was here, she might be side-tracked. She closed her eyes and drifted off to sleep within minutes.

LIAM HELPED Hank and Taz prepare the report on the mission and then get their gear together before they headed to the airport. The two were zipping up their bags, when the conference room door opened and Clayton Reid walked in followed by Sam Jensen.

"You son of a—" Liam went after Sam, but Taz and Hank grabbed him and held him back, but it didn't stop his fight to get free of them.

Sam held up his hands. "Hey man, I know you're upset, but I've been undercover. If you don't believe me, ask Reid here."

"It's true, Liam. Jensen works for the FBI just like I do."

"You man handled Simone. I saw the bruises on her arm."

"Bruises that will fade away, man. Better than if I beat her and broke a rib or something worse. I was the better choice for the abduction, but I couldn't be there the whole time. Lincler had me doing something else."

"You tried to recruit me for Lincler."

"And I would have made sure you failed the medical exam just like Billy Jennings. Besides, you weren't serious about working for Lincler. You were there snooping for information. I let you snoop. You think I didn't see you come out of the men's room and go down that corridor looking around? Why do you think I took you on a tour of the facility down there? Shipping and receiving wasn't part of a typical recruiting visit."

Liam stopped pulling against Taz and Hank. "I still should hit you or something. It would make me feel better."

"Have at it if it would." Sam held his arms wide for him to come at him.

"I might bruise my knuckles." He glanced down at his

hands now that Taz and Hank had released him. "Are you even married?"

"Nah. You know me, always been single. Danielle's a friend who posed for the photos so I could have a cover story. She also comes to town if I have a function that she needs to attend."

Liam shook his head. "I still don't understand the whole Lincler deal and the gang in Chicago. Why'd did the gang come to the Pied Piper and kill the bar tender?"

"I sold them bad weapons," Reid spoke up. "I used a division of Lincler to bring them into the country then distribute them. The gang in Chicago was pissed because they spent money on faulty weapons so they went after my daughter."

"Then Lincler got involved and decided to recoup their losses against Reid by luring Samwell Brady into a bogus deal with Testerman International. As soon as that went down, Testerman vanished." Jensen grinned.

"Okay, but how does Whittenbrier floating in the Chicago River play into all of this or is that just a coincidence?"

"Nothing is ever a coincidence when a man ends up dead," Reid said.

"Lincler and Whittenbrier were silent partners," Jensen said. "However, Whittenbrier didn't want to stay silent any longer. Lincler didn't want the change and he was afraid Whittenbrier would squeal in retaliation."

"As dirty as he was? I don't see that happening."

"I didn't either, but when you are power hungry like Lincler, you're looking down a very narrow pathway and paranoia can set in."

Liam nodded. "This whole cat and mouse game has ended with two fatalities. I hope it has been worth it."

"Two?" Reid and Jensen said in unison.

"Yeah. The bartender at the Pied Piper bar where Simone and her friends were last Friday night. He was shot by the gang members when they robbed the place. He died needlessly."

"What happened in Chicago is on the gang. We can't help what went down while we were trying to bring Lincler down," Reid said. "And whether Chicago PD goes after the gang for their crime or not is up to them. We've done our part."

Yeah, you've done your part. Made a mess of it.

He wasn't sure if he liked Simone's father's business tactics or what he was doing for the FBI. Likewise, Jensen working for the FBI as well made him question the guy's scruples. But there wasn't anything he could do about it. What was done was done, and he had to accept things as they were.

Jensen and Reid said goodbye and Liam walked Hank and Taz down to the lobby where they had a car coming to pick them up for the airport.

"Thank you both again for traveling all the way to help me out in a jam," Liam said. "Tell Hannah and Sadie I appreciate them both allowing you to come."

"Allowing us?" Taz said. "No, man. Hannah doesn't allow me to do anything. I decide what missions I go on. When and where I go. It was part of our marriage vows. Unspoken, but part of them."

"That's right, Bro." Hank slapped him on the back. "Sadie understands this line of work and she knows that when the job calls, we're on the next plane out. Even though I typically stick closer to home so I can be with her and Emma. But that is my choice, not hers."

"Yeah. I hear you both. Keep telling yourselves that," Liam said, walking outside of the hotel with them and waiting by the curb while they got into their ride. "Have a safe trip back to Montana."

CHAPTER 17

SIMONE WOKE to her alarm the next morning, not believing she'd slept all night without waking up. She turned the noise off, took her phone with her as she went to the bathroom, and sent Colleen a text to let her know she was thinking of her. She combed through her bed ragged hair and brushed her teeth to get rid of the horrible taste in her mouth before going back to the bedroom.

"You not going to work today?" Liam asked.

"I don't have to go to work today," she told him.

"You don't?"

"Nope. I talked to Cranston when I got back to the hotel yesterday and Webster-Reynolds is satisfied with what I have done already this week. They don't want to see me again until next year."

"So you made this trip for one day's work with them?"

"Technically it would have been more if I hadn't gotten ill or been abducted, but yes."

He snorted.

"What's so funny?"

"Civilian work."

She ignored him and opened up the drawer to the bedside table, taking out the padded room service menu. "I'm ordering food. I haven't eaten since Tuesday and I'm starving. Do you want anything?"

"You."

"Well, that is not on this menu. Try again."

"You drizzled in syrup?"

"Again, not on the menu."

"I give up. What do they have?" He sat up, looking over her shoulder.

She rattled off the choices and prices.

"That's not even funny. Get dressed. We're going to Oliver's."

"Where is that?"

"A little place the concierge told me about on Monday. Great food and atmosphere. We'll eat and be back in no time or we can do a little sightseeing while we're out."

"Nice," she said. "Oh, before I forget, we're having dinner with mom and Leland tonight."

"Where?"

"She didn't say, but I'll give her a call later this morning to find out."

"I'm looking forward to meeting your step-dad. He has to be an improvement over your dad."

"Liam!"

"Sorry, but I find your dad and his part in this whole Lincler business annoying. He is FBI, did he tell you that?"

"Not completely. But I put two and two together."

"I guess it rubs me raw to know he put your life in

danger to set Lincler up using the Chicago gang who tried retaliating against him going after you. And who paid for it? Phil, the bartender. And I don't even know the man, know nothing about him."

"He was nice. He was nice to Carly," Simone said. "He was married. He had a wife, so there is a widow."

"Damn." Liam pulled her to him.

THE REMAINDER of the day was spectacular, in Simone's opinion. Seeing the city with Liam was great and having dinner with her mom and Leland at their favorite bistro that evening was even better. Her mom had pulled her aside and asked if there was something going on between her and Liam and she had nodded. For once, her mom had clapped her hands together and smiled, approving of the man she'd picked. Maybe this was a good sign.

She felt like she was floating on air when they got back to the hotel suite. Liam let them into the room and she kicked off her heels before running into the bathroom. When she came out he was sitting on the sofa reading something on his phone. He was frowning.

"What's wrong?" She hurried over and curled up next to him.

"That bartender's funeral was today in Chicago. There was gunshots and an explosion in the parking lot. No one was injured, thank God, but Carly and Brand were there. Hawkeye just sent me a text."

"Oh my God. Poor Carly. When will this nightmare end for her?"

"I'm glad we're going back tomorrow. I need to be

there for my team, now that I know that you are potentially out of danger."

"Am I?"

"Yeah, Hawkeye just informed me that the gang member that they had in custody was murdered in his cell this morning."

"What? How did that happen?"

"They aren't sure yet. There's an investigation to see if it was an inside job, you know a hired hit, by a rival gang or what."

Simone laid her head on his shoulder, running her hand up and down his arm. "No one is really safe are they? We think we are, but we just never know."

"It's the world we live in."

"I don't like it very much at times."

"We just have to strive to make it a better place by being better people."

"I suppose." She rose to her feet and reached out her hand to him. "Come, let's go be better together."

"We'll be more than better, we'll be fantastically awesome together, sweetheart." He took her hand and pulled her to him, capturing her mouth with his, hungrily kissing her.

Simone melted against him. "You know when I said I wanted to be casual?"

He nodded.

"Forget that. There is nothing casual about us."

Liam threw his head back and held his hands up. "Thank God!"

She laughed and he scooped her up in his arms, carrying her into the bedroom.

EPILOGUE

THE PLANE RIDE BACK to Chicago was tortuous. Simone couldn't wait to touch down and get back to her apartment, drop her luggage off and go see Carly. Liam had tried repeatedly to get ahold of Brand without any luck and Commander Burns had been unreachable.

As soon as they got into the airport, Liam's phone started pinging with text messages. They stopped in the waiting area for him to check them before going to collect their baggage.

"Forget going to your apartment first. We're heading to Chicago Med. Brand's been injured."

"Oh no! Is it serious? Was he shot? Was Carly with him? What about Carly?"

"Whoa, sweetheart. Give me a second to answer your questions. Carly wasn't with him from what Will is telling me. She's at the hospital with Hawkeye. So we will go join them there."

"Okay." Simone felt her chest begin to constrict and her breathing become shallow again. She leaned forward and put her head between her knees until the blood flow ran to her head and she could breathe normal again.

Liam rubbed her back. "Did you take your pill this morning?"

"Yes. But it's still too soon since I started taking them. I still have reactions like this to news of this nature."

"Do you think you can slowly raise up? I'll go get you some water."

"I don't want water. I want to go see Carly …and Brand of course. I want to make sure our friends are safe." She smiled and squeezed his hand, silently praying for the day this all was put behind them and she could live a normal life again. If that could ever happen.

Liam called their driver at the PD and he was there to get them by the time they collected their baggage. Then they were on their way to Chicago Med. No matter how Simone was feeling, she made sure she came off as Miss Ray of Sunshine to her friends as soon as she got to the hospital.

"Carly! Jules!" Simone squealed and it echoed around the private waiting area of Chicago Med as she entered the doorway with Liam right behind her.

Carly turned and so did Jules. But then from the far right in the seating area, Simone saw someone she hadn't seen since college.

"Oh. My. Gawd," a brunette said, getting to her feet. "Simone Reid."

"Margot Wills!"

Simone left Liam and she practically ran to meet up with Margot in the middle of the room. They shared their favorite French kiss-kiss on each cheek, and then Margot took a long look at Will and Liam up and down.

"Burnsie," Margot said, turning to the commander, pointing to the men with her index finger. "Can you get me one of these?"

"Yeah, Commander Burns, she really needs one of these," Simone chimed in, "to keep *her* out of trouble."

The man looked baffled by the request and he tinged red around the collar. "No. And double no. I should have known the two of you knew one another. You're too much alike."

Margot and Simone giggled, hugging one another. Linking arms, they walked over to the two-seater and sat down to talk.

"So what have you been up to, Margot? I lost touch with you after graduation when you went to Paris for that internship."

Margot rolled her eyes. "Oh that. It ended and I stayed for three months more because I considered myself a Parisian by then. However, the Senator wasn't having any of it. He begged me to come home. So I did. It's so great to see you again. First I'm reconnected with Carly and now you. Of course there is Jules here, but she hasn't bothered to say hello since she walked in with her hunky guy. And she probably won't. We never were that much on speaking terms."

"You could change that," Simone suggested.

"And break with tradition?" Margot shook her head. "That might upset status quo."

Simone giggled. "I've missed you, Margot."

. . .

LIAM WATCHED as Simone chatted with the woman across the room and half listened to what Will was saying to Hawkeye about not being able to reach Brand on his cellphone all week.

"I haven't been able to since last Saturday either," he said.

"I've had no trouble," Hawkeye said. "Have either of you heard from Kincaid?"

They both nodded.

"I know for a fact that Brand hasn't heard from him either," Carly offered. "We discussed it on the way to my job interview. He was worried about all his men because they'd been silent."

"Carly mentioned this when Jules and I arrived so that's why I asked Donovan about it," Will said.

"Do you think someone has tampered with his phone?" Liam asked.

Hawkeye shook his head. "It's unlikely. He's been around very few people other than Kevin Petree and Carly all week."

"Don't forget Ragsdale," Carly said.

"But were Brand and the P.I. alone for any period of time for the man to have access to Brand's phone?" Hawkeye asked.

Carly shook her head.

"What about Petree? Did you ever see Brand lay his phone down when Petree was around?"

"No, but I wasn't with them when Brand and Kevin went shopping for his suit. Kevin took him to the places he usually went and I stayed at the apartment. I can't imagine that he'd do anything to harm us. He's been so great all week."

"I'm not saying the man is guilty, I'm looking at the possibilities of who had access to Brand's phone. I'll get a tech guy down here to examine it and make sure it hasn't been tampered with so we will know for sure why the signals have been crossed."

HOURS PASSED and it was after midnight before Carly was able to go to the ER to see Brand. When she returned, she reported that he was awake and responsive. She'd even spoken to the doctor and had a good report on Brand.

"The kick boxing blow caused agitation to the phrenic nerve due to the hit near the diaphragm. The doctor believes he'll be fine. He was very lucky. There were no broken ribs."

Liam let out the breath he had been holding since Carly started talking.

"When can we see him?"

"Tomorrow? I'm afraid he's gone back to sleep now. Sorry. I know you and Will have been waiting a long time for news and a chance to see him."

"Don't be sorry, Carly. We'll see him tomorrow," Will said.

"Sure. He needs his rest tonight. Tomorrow is soon enough," Liam agreed.

"There is one more piece of news. I'm not sure if Brand would want me to share it or not," Carly said, "but the shrapnel in his chest has moved. He can now have surgery to get it out, but he doesn't want it. At least not right now because of recovery time."

"What? But that is what kept him from returning to the SEALs." Will bounced back and forth on the balls of his feet. "Doesn't he realize what chance he's been given?"

"He does…at least he says he does."

"Ultimately it is Brand's choice." Liam got it. He looked over where Simone sat still talking with the brunette. "I think we'll head out."

"Okay. Thank you for coming." Carly gave him a hug.

Liam walked over to where Simone was and held out his hand to her. She took it and stood, looking back at her friend.

"I'll see you around, Chicca."

The brunette eyed him. "You have her tamed. You must be something special."

Simone giggled. "I never kiss and tell."

"Since when?" the brunette asked.

"Yeah, since when?" Carly asked, taking Simone's place on the two seater.

"Since I have Don Juan in my life."

ABOUT LEANNE TYLER

Award-winning author Leanne Tyler writes sweet and somewhat sensual romances whether historical, contemporary, or romantic suspense. Her newest series the Chicago Protection Task Force is part of the Brotherhood Protection World. Other series includes her popular The Good Luck series--a collection of short contemporary romantic comedy romances set in East Tennessee. In addition to her contemporary novels, she writes American historical novels set prior to and during the Civil War.

Leanne lives in East Tennessee with her son. For more information about her books and to sign up for her newsletter, please visit leannetyler.com.

ORIGINAL BROTHERHOOD PROTECTORS SERIES

BY ELLE JAMES

Brotherhood Protectors Series

ABOUT ELLE JAMES

ELLE JAMES also writing as MYLA JACKSON is a *New York Times* and *USA Today* Bestselling author of books including cowboys, intrigues and paranormal adventures that keep her readers on the edges of their seats. With over eighty works in a variety of sub-genres and lengths she has published with Harlequin, Samhain, Ellora's Cave, Kensington, Cleis Press, and Avon. When she's not at her computer, she's traveling, snow skiing, boating, or riding her ATV, dreaming up new stories. Learn more about Elle James at www.ellejames.com

Website | Facebook | Twitter | GoodReads | Newsletter | BookBub | Amazon

Follow Elle!
www.ellejames.com
ellejames@ellejames.com

 facebook.com/ellejamesauthor
twitter.com/ElleJamesAuthor